GRAFFITI ON THE WALLS OF MY MIND

Lorna D Whitfield

Graffiti On The Walls Of My Mind

Copyright © 2024 Lorna D Whitfield
All rights reserved.
No reproductions of any kind, way, shape,
form or fashion without the
written permission of the author.

ISBN: 979-8-218-36099-3

Cover Artist: Shardae Simpson
YKYB Studio   Instagram: ykybstudio

DEDICATED

TO ANCESTRAL SPIRITS
that Converged as Forces of Nature
to Deliver Us from Bondage
into the Promise of Freedom

<u>To All Those That Have Lost Loved Ones To Violence</u>
to the Parents that look to the horizon for the *child*
    that will never come home
to those that still feel the warmth of sharing a moment,
    a touch, a kiss with a loving *soul mate*
to the Children that were robbed of the *love, strength*
    and guidance that only a Parent can give them
    on their *walk* through life
<u>Not Left Behind</u>   <u>Still Here to Love and Prosper</u>

    Joseph Emil Baker   Mentor and Best Friend
Brotherly love and encouragement gave me the confidence to push through barriers in pursuit of my dreams. Motivational expertise inspired me and others to think outside the box. His mission: a safe space to exchange ideas and focus on the importance of teamwork to achieve WIN-WIN outcomes. Joe's philosophy of life will live on in family, friends and the people touched by his unique approach to life and spiritual enlightenment.

DISCLAIMER

All references to race, color and creed listed herein are for the sole purpose of adhering to status quo conversational norms
NOT to Validate them

A Matter Of Personal Perspective
Some Content May Be Offensive

Some of this information may trigger **PTSD**
emotional despair   headaches   disgust   confusion
disbelief   nightmares   depression   insomnia   night sweats
<u>*Due To*</u>   **complicity**   **self-reflection**   **denial**   **victimization**

The opinions expressed in this book represent the sole views of the author and not necessarily any person or organization listed.

Stated or inferred corruption, implied criminality, human rights violations are directed at those guilty, by law or through complicity. It is not meant to accuse, condemn or malign any other person, business, bureau, or organization.

Names, events, references, statistics can be referenced through a broad range of public search engines, written documentation and personal accounts that may still be available.

*be inspired   explore further   join the conversation
the Truth will reveal itself*

check here   ☐ I am a HUMANE human being   if applicable

K E Y to understanding:

(MOC)	Men of Color	(WOC)	Women of Color
(BLM)	Black Lives Matter	(COC)	Children of Color
(POC)	People of Color	(BIPOC)	Black & Indigenous POC
(BP)	Black people	(INA)	Indigenous Native American
(AA)	African American	(WP)	white privilege
(NHI)	No Human Involved	(ICWA)	Indian Child Welfare Act

PREFACE

(Read the **Back Cover** 1st Before Proceeding)

The quest for white supremacy spawned a draconian law that classified People of Color (POC) as <u>aliens</u>. Even though America rated POC as a *red level* threat, this classification was upgraded to 3/5 of a human being. LIEs that fostered injustice altered the social evolution of millions of non-white people for generations.

People of Color seeking justice, relief from oppression precipitated the drafting of US Laws and Regulations that would neutralize any threat to white majority rule. Diabolical acts committed by white privilege to acquire massive wealth, power, property was protected as legal and justified.

Extremism was used to recruit and indoctrinate white followers into a society driven by prejudice. The buy-in became so profitable, RACISM transcended being a system, to become an institution.

And Here We Are
>embroiled in a doctrine that preserves the integrity of one *species* of human beings while defiling and dehumanizing all others.

>**What could've been, what would've been, but for a racist society** *so spellbound* **by self-preservation and self-indulgence, the cost of committing ethnic genocide was of no consequence.**

CONTENTS

SECTION I

    a. Copyright page
    b. Dedication page
    c. Disclaimer
    d. Preface
    e. Contents
    f. Acknowledgements
    g. Introduction

SECTION II

    a. ETCHINGS   The Talk………………………………………..1
    b. Epilogue……………………………………………………..137
    c. About the Author…………………………………………..139
    d. Other Literary Works……………………………………..141

ACKNOWLEDGEMENTS

Carrie   Elijah Sansom
My parents created a hedge of protection around me as a child and provided a safety net as an adult to be used *only*, in extreme distress. They instilled a 'tow the line' philosophy that makes me mentally stronger every day.

Pamela Brown   sister   Juanita Parker   best friend
confidants always there to listen critique guide   comfort

LaVashia Whitfield   daughter Sasha   (Larry Taylor)
my ROCK   entrepreneur   loving mother
Reginald Hatcher, Jr   grandson Reggie
entering manhood with a new appreciation for family, 'eye on the prize' and love of life
Krystal Tamra daughters   intelligent spiritual loving mothers that will always have my heart
Everlasting love and blessings to my grand, great and G2 grand children   Godchild (Aryanna)

Amani   Alexander Brown, jr   niece and nephew
the duo of cool calm collected   living life to its fullest

Linda Rice   sister
caring   extraordinary talent   immeasurable enthusiasm
George Rice III   nephew   joyful inspired gifted

Elijah Thorne Sansom   brother
no-nonsense approach to 'Just Get It Done'
my 1st publishing agent

Robert Bates and family   more beloved *Son,* than cousin

Marie Baker and family   everyone's chosen mother   sister spiritual host of unwavering strength and love

Family & Forever Friends   Kindred spirits

Sansom   Scales   Whitfield   Caruthers   Wanda Loving/Watkins   Baker   Holmes   Cora Williams   Muzahem & Madonna Alsayaf   Greg Head   Jonathan Ward   Irene & Max Igol   Luvone Smith   Leroy Sims   Delores & Lorenzo Hayes   John Brown   Roland Crosby   Inez Smith (Ms Smooth)   Waynette Sims   Carol Ratliff   Melanie & Alexander Robinson   Majida Kinnard   Trudy & Raymond Langley   Shannette Slaughter

DETROIT POINTS OF INTEREST:
    Charles Wright African American Museum
    James & Grace Lee Boggs Center
    Motown Museum
    Joe Louis Fist
    Detroit Riverwalk
    Heidelberg Project
    DABLS MBAD African Bead Museum
    Belle Isle Detroit
    International Bridges   Ambassador   Gordie Howe
    Detroit-Windsor Tunnel

INTRODUCTION

Capitalism   Racism   GREED*ism*

Capitalism breeds *Greed,* injecting the venom of corruption into every crack and crevice of a receptive society. Slaves were brought to the New World as property to serve or die in a perverted sphere of white power influence that rooted and flourished.

The Separate but Unequal airborne virus in America soon became a pandemic of RACISM. The **first** POLICE*ing* Patrols in America were formed for the **sole** purpose of providing security services for *human* traffickers. Slave owners deployed self-righteous, depraved, malcontents to serve as bounty hunters to retrieve freedom seekers. These mobs of disgruntled flag waving, bible toting vigilantes were granted legal authority to track, buy, sell, punish, and imprison People of Color. Slave exploitation was operated with autonomy because the FOX was the **C**hief **E**xecutive **O**fficer of the HEN HOUSE.

This pool of humans was farmed out to the
US government, industrial and private sector
businesses as an unpaid labor force.

Today's adaptations, not so far off the mark

Slavery, cloaked in a veil of privilege, was not new. However, sadism in America elevated cruelty, *beyond the pale*.

A not so simple Truth
Slaveowners held extravagant dinner parties for 10-20 guest on immaculate estate lawns. Sumptuous feasts were served to family, friends, and guest in formal attire by Black servants in regal dress.

Main attraction; a shirtless colored **man** hanging by his wrist. Above a pool of blood, he was whipped mercilessly, during a 5-course gourmet meal. The screaming and moaning waned, during the consumption of exotic desserts.
   The *coup de grâce*, ***death!*** *Smelling salts anyone?*

ETCHINGS *The TALK*

What is it like for POC N America **Still**
Take a Seat on the Receiving End of the Experience
No chronology   just crisscrossing Black History's timeline

Manichaeism	21st century
Mani Apostle of Light	scientific studies
a **mere** man	corroborate
deemed a prophet	the fact **RACE**
in 3rd century Babylon	is a fallacy
encapsulated	human beings are
multiple religions	ONE SPECIES
into a single ideology	genetically
symbolized by	all humans are
Light vs Dark	*99.9 %* identical
ushered in	DNA with
the seeds of racism	dark melanin
	confirmed to be the
<u>light</u> good true pure	oldest known
beautiful superior	
<u>dark</u> bad false sinister	I Am YOU
repugnant inferior	YOU Are ME

Greed *Racial animus enshrouds The Mind like a layer of decayed skin   poisoning every thought conjured **within***

<u>1 drop</u> Black blood   Jim Crow classification of African
    American bloodline as unworthy   subhuman
<u>Blood Quantum rule</u>   attempt to eradicate the lineage
    of Indigenous Native Americans

The **FALLACY**
  multiple human species   races   white superior race
  negligible contributions by POC in Americas prosperity

The **FEAR**
white superior species	*eradicated*
wp crimes exposed	*prosecuted*
white hatred lust 4 POC	*turned to love marriage*
ALL humans	*constitutional rights enforced*
Wp generational wealth	*at risk*

The **REALITY**
  accountability justice reparations *for*
tyranny	immoral acts against humanity
criminal liability	genocide
*socio*economic loss	misappropriation
racial disparity	mass incarceration bias
eminent domain abuses	property loss destruction

POC   classified as inferior subhuman species
in manipulated scientific data
published by renown 18th century anthropologist[s]
with superiority complex

Ergo   today[s] moral judgements   tainted attitudes
targeting BIPOC for all of societies depravity

mass incarceration ***$80 billion industry***
Quid Pro Quo *swap* meet to entrap MOC into a cycle of
recidivism   *infinite* pool of unpaid labor   ***aka slavery***

What is your Philosophy Of LIFE

optimism   pessimism
live   let live
Mine over Mindfulness

systemic racism could have targeted
blue   green   hazel eyes
the *short   tall   fat   thin*

1ˢᵗ human originated
2.5 million years ago
East Africa
from Australopithecus

ancestors proved POC are formidable opponents against adversity when cultural awareness character is infused with fortitude

Whoop Whoop
On the Mark

the concept of
RACE was
set in motion
to justify Mans
inhumanity to
a chosen color
of Man

Golden truth
exposing the Tip
of the ice**Berg**

<u>CRITICAL RACE THEORY</u>
examines Civil Rightˢ and laws that protect them

proposed mandatory school curriculums will identify **unadulterated** facts that all of mankind originated from Africans with dark melatonin

EVE Gene   **mtDNA**   **AFRICA**
<u>Origin of **ALL** humans   born last 200,000yrs</u>

I'm not going to just let you kill my Sons

Great Grandmothers Battle Cry

1841 Extraordinary Popular <u>Delusions</u>
and the <u>Madness</u> of Crowds
by Charles MacKay

Crowd psychology drives numerous acts of violence
National Delusions   Peculiar Follies
Psychological Delusions

Crowd psychology can create an emotional
feedback loop whereby dissent might be stifled
as the crowd not wanting to miss out
hears only what they want

whole communities suddenly fix their minds upon
one subject   going MAD in its pursuit
millions of people simultaneously excited
with one delusion

<u>lynchings   insurrection   town burnings   war atrocities</u>

FLORIDA   1900s
DOZIER
Reform School

Auction Block   Chattel slavery
prime specimens   *livestock*
Negro men   women   children
branded by previous owners
grease tar covered wounds

THEY were *special*
To Someone

Sometimes I just...
Can Not **catch my breath**

American **L**egislative **E**xchange **C**ouncil
<u>National</u> policy making organization
<u>peer **elected** Task force</u>   pays fee to sit at the table
corporate | ***create*** the Bill structure that
private sector | *dictates public policy*
politicians | *including terms that protect*
lobbyists | *respective business interest*

BILLS   are then introduced on the floor by
<u>chosen</u> State Legislators

ALEC exposed.org   <u>*unpaid labor*</u>

POC   have **long** been the caretakers of **wp**
<u>children   houses   food prep   health   property   land
without</u> *wp* lifting a finger   <u>without</u> the benefit of
Readn   Writn   Rithmetic   book learn n

SO which RACE inept stupid lazy undisciplined

different when <u>you</u> read it   HUH

N word
original definition
Oxford English
dictionary
ignorant person

no reference to
skin color

SIMPLY ☑ American

STAND YOUR GROUND Bill
catapulted into
<u>LAW</u> by **private club**
see ALEC

5

Overt Racism
social consensus to
solicit HATE
induce anxiety   fear
incite violence

POC   portrayed as
*deformed
maniacal caricatures*
super predators
enemies of the state
mulatto mongrels
drug addicts
other asinine
references to
propagate the fallacy
of <u>superior</u>ity

SPIRITUALITY

HOUSE OF
WE CAN

13th Amendment
Civil Rights
*except for convicted
criminals*

employment
barrier to aid
recidivism by
preserving a
stocked pig pen

MASS INCARCERATION
*covert OP
for the NEW slavery*

Ocmulgee Mounds Macon GA

SEL<u>F</u> doubt
Los<u>E</u>
<u>A</u>
Pa<u>R</u>alysis

VOTE   **Julius Perry**
<u>***Died***</u>   *trying*

CoreCivic
formerly   CCA
Corrections Corporation
of America

OWN   Manage
**private prisons
detention centers**

paid for seat on **ALEC**
Task Force

BLACK PEOPLE   RULED KINGDOMS
Kings   Queens   BC   to   present day   POTUS
PHAROAHS   Dynasty XXV of Egypt   744BC
Emperors & Empresses   1889 – 1974
Children of   King Solomon   Queen of Sheba
<u>Excelling through history as</u>   Architect   Philosopher
Empire *builder*   Mama   Daddy   Secret *Service*
Scientist   Ceramist   Network *owner*   Textile *artist*
Chemist   Abolitionist   Artist   Real Estate owner
Musician   Human   Nurse   Jockey   Doctor
Nobel *laureate*   Metalworker   Comedian
Inventor   Quilter   Aviator   Cowboy
Geologist   Educator   Blacksmith   Carpenter
Attorney *General*   Banker   Sports *legend*   Model
Graphic *artist*   Mathematician   Editor   Technician
Choreographer   Baker   Author   Actor   Orator
Publisher   Toolmaker   TV host   Conservationist
Stone *Mason*   Weaver   Gold medalist   Milliner
Engineer   Veterinarian   Dancer   Military *Officer*
Singer   Aeronautic Engineer   Playwright
Radio personality   network owner   Farmer
Basket Maker   Cosmetologist   Poet   Automaker
Lawmakers   Aesthetician   Astronomer   Brickmaker
Symphony *director*   Movie *director*   Author
Photographer   Skilled *Tradesman*   Animal *husbandry*
Apparel *designer*   Wood*smith*   Anthropologist
Leatherworker   Valedictorian   Spiritual *leader*
Executive   Horse *trainer*   Potter   Producer
Cinematographer   Hockey Pro   Billionaire
Surveyor   Biologist   Entrepreneur   Composer
Deep *Sea Diver*   Law *enforcement*   Oceanographer
Bodybuilder   Life Coach   Politician   Wood Carver
Botanist   Alpine Skier   Candlestick maker
Suffragette   *Chef*   Auto Designer   etc…

<u>INFO</u> **excluded from Mandatory School Curriculums**

SARAH BAARTMAN
1789 to 1815
Hottentot Venus
Black Venus

African descendants
Ndongo WCA   Kabasa
were here 1500[S]
B4 English colonist
slave ships   1492
1619   White Lion
Treasurer
1783   Zong

Golden Age
of KUSH
KANDAKES
**African
Warrior
Queens**
independently
wealthy
Omnificent

#1600   Mechanic
travel ID   Slave Badge

#1600 Pennsylvania Ave
*Him POTUS   Her VPOTUS
Rulers of the free world*

Black Wallstreet   Paradise Theater   Harlem Club
Black Broadway   Paradise Valley   Hastings Street
Cotton Club   Apollo   Black Bottom
destroyed by wp   intervention   malfeasance

Kidnapped
slaves Of
Madagascar

ill[S] of Captivity
High blood pressure   Diabetes
Heart disease   Migraines
Depression   Anxiety
Low *self* esteem   Obesity
Drug Addition   Suicide
PTSD   distrust of justice system

Worldwide Demand For Civil Rights
                  Social strategies to right the wrong
<u>overseas</u>   **everyone** ➤ civil unrest   rebellion revolt

<u>In America</u> **wp**   armed patriots   right to protest
               POC   terrorist uprising   **rioters**

Ancient Africa   *racially homogeneous*

   the Myth ~~Sambo~~   topple the Iron Curtain
The <u>Reality</u> POTUS   of prejudice
          VPOTUS   IN America

                      A TEST

ORIGIN of TERM	
race	white black people
caucasian	POC
species of human	cholo
white supremist	slavery
black devil	white devil
good ole boy	haole ^eha
DEFINE TERM	
black *afro* American	white *afro* American
white privilege	black Asian
euro American	colored European
indigenous white people	brown people
racial disparity	*interracially mixed*
white people	black culture
ginger	copperheads
assimilation	oppression

We do not want to just anticipate CHANGE
WE WANT TO KNOW JUSTICE

Author   J A Villacorta

Africans preceded
Columbus by
centuries
<u>introduced their own</u>
political systems
religious traditions
to the New World

Aryan Race
NO
anthropological
historical
archeological
<u>*evidence*</u> of
existence

American **B**ail **C**oalition
pay bail bondsman   10% non refundable fee

choices   wait for trial rotting in jail   plea deal

Selling Off Our Freedom   Color of Change ACLU.org

Automatic weapons Kill **faster**

Five O   is a
TV term

IT BEARS REPEATING *to ad nauseam*

We have interracial children
We ***do not see*** <u>color</u>   <u>race</u>

you cannot unsee <u>color</u>   their Lives are in peril
constraints on freedom stem from racial profiling
claiming otherwise is simply denial

Igbo Landing   mass suicide   FRANK
SLAVERY **rejec**ted *to death*   E
Underground Railroad   M
March 4 freedom   B
BLM protest   R
NO Justice   NO Peace   E
                                               E

Black females   **VPOTUS**
Supreme Court Justice

                              It took a Village
                          to slay Frankenstein
US CONSTITUTION   he was *oblivious*
the THEM *US* version   to the fact that
post it prominently   he was a Monster
on the WAILING   WALL   but *THEY* KNEW

Loved Ones   LOST
bones scattered along   LINCOLN
  highways   byways   HEIGHTS
graves beneath   OHIO
overgrown fields
  decaying stumps of
    strange fruit trees
                            B nice   B kind
we must raise   B grateful
the roof against   show gratitude
clandestine alliances   B inclusive
that impede   Celebrate U
accountability   Cherish others

Mental Illness   Murder   **Michael Brown**
Kenneth Chamberlain
White Plains NY   2011   FERGUSON MO
                                     under siege
LaVashia just cried   **3** Warrants
                                     per household

SUPPORT   HBCU^S   Charitable foundations
Black enterprise   Female businesses

Black men are **6.5%** of the USA population
40.2% of the jail population   I in 3
<u>more</u> in jail than ALL *known slaves* in 1850

build the houses *mansions*	**U** canNOT reside there
plow fields tend the *land*	**U** canNOT own IT
Harvest the crop	**U** canNOT eat the bounty
Market the products	**U** canNOT share any profit

conversational posturing   attaching blame
relocation   not even reparations   can quell ***trauma***
IS miss iss ippi   ***still burn*** ing

African <u>Males</u>   <u>Females</u> *chained shackled* **killed** in
Transatlantic slave ship purgatory ***Children included***

POLICE Medical Alert **update**

CHOKING   heart lungs working improperly
   starved of oxygen
      carbon dioxide gases mixed with fluid
        fluid buildup around both organs cells
       light pink or *blood* tinted mucus
      uncontrollable vomiting

  central nervous system *non* responsive
   foaming at the mouth resulting in
   asphyxiation   *coma*   *death*

    wp private property owners erect illegal
adjacent barriers which prevent access to **public**
    waterways oceanic views beaches trails

Dictatorship under the guise of Colonization
  Colonization under the guise of Spiritual enrichment
  Spiritual enrichment with the caveat of blind allegiance
            INDOCTRINATION

      George Wallace   **the funny in Serious**

for centuries interracial sex was against the law
MOC were lynched for *looking* at a white woman
white males raped   disfigured black woman   girls
    with no moral or legal consequence

       I am not going to just let you kill my Son[s]

self sufficient INA nations governed by
tribal councils holistic approach
to the sanctity of wildlife sky water land
not ignorant blood thirsty savages
as vilified in media books on stage screen

<u>Scourge of the West</u>
would better describe white vigilante settlers
lawless bureaucrats military fanatics
deplorable hired guns that blazed across the
country from East to West ravaging
people land homesteads the environment
LIKE A SWARM OF LOCUST

MAJOR TAYLOR
fastest
in the world

5 subdivisions
of Homo Sapiens
Myths & Lies

young Henry was on the wrong side of the track
darkness had fallen before he could get back
avoiding the terror that could impede his travels
he reached home by blending into the shadows
his duty to family now defined by great need
would strengthen his commitment to succeed
vowing to never meet his *Maker* lying face down
like Daddys maimed body in a backwater town

Indian scholar Rafique Jairazbhoy
African explorers in the New World
19th dynasty era
Masters of their Own Destiny

You Feel Me Now

```
B R       N  A
 *  E  N    *
  T    O   R
   A     O
       Y L
```

TRIGGERS for BP **PTSD**

micro   maxi   aggression
police brutality
employment barriers
tap dancing   black face
videos of racial abuse
inferior products   services
intolerance   ridicule
blatant disrespect from
complacent   onlookers

**The Great Dying
of 1492**
overzealous
sociopaths
devised
their <u>strategy</u>
to create a new
white Christian
civilization

private prisons charge
$30 to $200 per day
of your tax money
to house 1 prisoner

what
extent of
*collateral
damage
shall
compel
us to
eradicate
the cause*

FED UP

R I P   now I lay me down to sleep
bullets shot blindly *ne^er* an official peep
it is my lawful right to protect
House   Home   MY LOVE
when under mortal threat

police officer killings   2013 to 2019
99% of officers never charged
police officer indicted   2nd° murder
18 complaints of misconduct
<u>the deal</u>   **two** letters of reprimand

> **US MILITARY GENERAL**
> Department of Justice
> Top Prosecutor duly sworn
> appointed   to uphold the **LAW**
> Protect Human   Civil Liberties
>
> publicly announces <u>full support to</u>
> re**Elect a public official he dubbed**
> a pathological liar
> prone to manic tirades
> having no impulse control
> <u>accused</u> of fraud   insurrection
> breaching proceedings of
> constitutional law
> collusion with foreign dictators
>
> while   adamantly declaring
> N<u>EVER</u> to work with the alleged
> criminal again
>
> <u>EXPLAIN</u> THAT   to the children

I
REST
MY

C
A
S
E
←

everyone
recognizes
racism

it is
everywhere

everyone
accepts
racism

**so it
prevails**

*Kindness spreads Joy
Godliness can only
manifest in a
giving heart
humble mind
welcoming hand*
CARE 2 CARE

BANJOS were **never**
<u>seen</u> before being
plucked from the
lap of a toe tapping
slave in 1800^s

EMMETT TILL	Corruption	8 min 48 sec
Cold Case Act	Antagonism	SIT IN
Of 2007	*Devil May*	or KNEEL
	Care ^tudes	Down
the _whistle_	are LEARNED	**around** the
from the North	BEHAVIORS	World
silenced		
in the South		

NBCC
National
Black
Business
Chamber

there are places we will not go
clearly places we can not go
there are places we do not want to go
there are places we go anyway
driving cross country   Russian roulette
the GREEN BOOK
for black folks   well*being*

white privilege   *means to an end*
    lynching   murder   rape   torture
  severe family ties   oppression   castration
mass incarceration   pillage   discrimination
    mutilation   depravity   desecration
        to achieve   Master*dom*

seems like OVERKILL   for **supreme** beings

civil disobedience   <u>infers</u> the act of resisting injustice
is a <u>criminal act</u>   it is in fact an exercise in <u>social reform</u>
to stop the clock long enough   to assess a lawless act
practice   policy detrimental to the **disenfranchised**

Woman are not the rib bone   but the *backbone*
of the sanctity of life   the ministers of *self* sacrifice
doctors of mercy   healing
the embodiment of selfless love

INA used rituals
medicinal herbs   spices
to *ward off* sickness
cure diseases   introduced
by foreign invaders

ICONIC   landmarks in
predominantly black
cities   whitewashed

national marketing
campaigns underrepresent
Black demographics

Wp <u>closet skeletons</u>
cloaked
corruption

<u>family   friends   associates</u>
pay to play collusion
public office conspirators
sex traffickers
drug   porn addicts
insurrectionist
terrorists
white supremist

OCOEE FLORIDA
M
A
S
S
A
C
R
E
1920

corporate corruption
rakes in more
illicit funds
per week
than street crimes
per annum

riches without toil are a
dopamine rush for <u>*MORE*</u>
<u>anything</u>   <u>everything</u>

NO restraint   character
or humanity to
suppress the MadNeSS

enjoy the day   enjoy life   count your blessings
show COMPASSION   BLESS *someone else*

catastrophic
CLIMATE CHANGES
aftermath of GREED

1st f*emale* Skilled Trades
<u>apprentice</u> electrician
GM Hydra Matic Division
22yr old single mother
victim of misogyny

extending a lifeline
will always
Hook a Mind
Save a SOUL

restroom break wo
permission along with
<u>other biased claims</u>
<u>resulted in months</u>
<u>off without income</u>

wages ***recovered*** thru
UAW grievances
work hour credits ***lost***
toward historic claim as
1st Black Female
<u>journeyman</u> electrician
milestone forever lost

New York Schomburg
Center for Research
in Black Culture

DO NOT settle for the ***upper level*** of <u>**lower class**</u>

hidden history of BIPOC has more *relevance*
in K to 12th grade American history studies then
mandatory Christopher Columbus   exploits
so too   Native American history needs revision
Nations of independent tribes   condensed
into a single image of drunken   illiterate   savages

Injustice against POC

THEN	→	NOW
slavery		mass incarceration
involuntary servitude		minimum wage
Jim Crow		convict leasing
vigilantes		police brutality
murder		same
voting rights denied		gerrymandering
deny loans insurance		redlining
inferior housing		slumlords
substandard public education		same
medical experimentation		inferior healthcare
food insecurity		same
taxation without representation		same
malicious attacks		same
complicit observers		same
segregation		separate but unequal
propaganda		social media global access
prejudice		racially biased media coverage
defamation		*micro* aggression
Civil Rights violations		same
no legal representation		*inept* public defenders

Ain^t NO BODY got Time for this MF
JENIFER LEWIS

MLB brothers **Fleetwood   Weldy Walker**

African **TREASURES**
stolen
Kingdom of Benin
P l a q u e s

POC on **MAX** display
by white privilege when
paid for testimonials
OR   *subject of disorder*

POC speak candidly about racial discrimination when
elderly   terminal   celebrity   *the latter   still risky*

POC
2 to 8 people
street battles
Go Viral

white privilege
organized crime
massacres
human trafficking
assassinations
where is Hoffa
suppressed
10000+ people
participate in
domestic terrorism
1000s never ID^d
video evidence
quietly archived

a tremendous amount
of mental prowess
stamina goes
n2 thwarting EVIL

ASK the
Capitol Hill Police

counter measures
taken against
Civil Liberty
infringement
should BE
rewarded
not censured

Stand Up   Stand Out

L O N G *Live*
Peace Keepers

FOREVER
Moving Forward

Women reclaim your natural leadership   <u>State of Grace</u>
a healing force to right the wrongs of moral disgrace
transcend differences to benefit the whole
family   society need you to be bold
servant in the community   respect in the home
children will carry the torch wherever they roam

JUSTICE DENIED

Kenosha Wisconsin
SAY THEIR NAMES

1865 POC
multi*year*
sentences
for
SpitTing
on the
ground

fight or flight a daily conundrum
sometimes it requires a family quorum
decisions can be deadly made in haste
a Mothers worst nightmare in any case
do I want to deal or just stay safely at home
creates social   economic issues of its own
lost opportunities on paths not tread
because of roadblocks in my head

African
Influence
dominated
the Mother
Culture
of Mexico

Olmec
civilization

POC   **THE TALK**
the odds are stacked

Police Stop   survival behaviors
walking or driving **24/7**
submissive body language
do not run   hands up
do not search for ID
registration   insurance info

an affront to wp authority
drives acts of *racial profiling*
skin with melanin   hoodie
facial features   ethnic attire
hair styles   gait   verbiage

society is conditioned to fear you
as a menace to society
an amoral contentious animal

**Negro
professors
taught in
the ancient
universities
of
Alexandria**

GREENWOOD   <u>C</u>aucasus <u>M</u>ountains
O   *multi* ethnic society
K   origin of caucasian
L   no skin color reference
A
H   white + white = white
O   SO <u>what color</u> were
M   the first people
A   1921   ON EARTH

911   Pandemic   Hurricane   Tornado   Fire

1st RESPONDERS   ESSENTIAL WORKERS

 BLESS YOU   FOREVER IN OUR HEARTS

OUR CHILDREN's LIVES   No One can hear U
are **MORE** *precious*   crying alone
then WRONGFUL   in an empty room
DEATH $$$$ **REACH OUT**
settlements   **SOMEONE** wants
     to Listen   Help

Just as the corner hooker is purported to be the
only option for illegal sex activity
so goes the LIE of neighborhood crack houses
having monopoly on ***dope*** distribution in America

invisible   Prior to the 1820s there
I AM NOT   were *more* Africans
HI Neighbor   than Europeans in America
     enslaved.org

Carried like *The Cross*
the stigma is like no other
human beings on earth
defined by skin color

false claims of superiority
since the 17th century
systemic racism
disrupted   Black mastery

all human beings are of
African descent
the **Mother**land demands
naysayers repent

5 ANCIENT Egypt
Black Pharaohs

Black race
 Kmt Kemet
  Kam Ham

some wounds *too* egregious
stitched up time can not seal the
ravages of *crime*

why does it have to be so *hard*
LOVE makes   LIFE so much
more enjoyable

children embrace   I C U 4 U
when unhindered by adult **prejudice**

Alabama National
Memorial for
Peace and Justice

Lynchings
800 listings
by County

BERBICE
Slave
Rebellion
1763

Traffic Etiquette
Before U freak out
check Ur blinkers
may not be work N

THE   GLASS
BOTTLE
R
E
E

On paint store
color palette
YOUR Skin
ISsssss

white privilege
profiteers considered
looting   maiming
dismemberment
within the scope of
enslaving POC

4 those that knew
4 those that
turned a deaf ear
4 those that ignored
oppression without
assigning blame
liability

<u>witness the reckoning</u>
FOUND human remains
retrieved documents
hidden scrolls
word of mouth accounts
attest to the
human death toll
property loss
  READ UP

DRUG Lords   Czars
live in towers
mega mansions
suburban enclaves
OWN <u>crime networks</u>
shipping fleets
conglomerates
islands
lobbyists
SLAVES

<u>NOT drug houses</u>

the nucleus
from which
strength
of character
emanates is
RESPECT

4 Little Girls   Forty Acres and a Mule Filmworks
faces of Angels   victims of War on Blackness
U hav seen   U hav mourned   but are U listening

U **CAN** make a change
U **CAN** make a difference

Malala Yousafzai
Cassidy **H**utchinson
The *Cuban* Effect   *m*

GRAFFITI
a visual
expression
of ***artistic***
internal
combustion

ThE Black Panthers
to a
Black *Panther King*
to a
Black Panther Nation

IF you can Dream it
you can Achieve it

mapping PREJUDICE
is a Head Game

straight poker
do not fold   CALL

people utilize only
10% of their
brain power

another MYTH to
DISSUADE   people
from realizing
their full potential

the majority of the
brain never rests
connections are cut
rerouted routinely

right brain   left brain
use it or lose it

NO Dignity   thrown down to kiss the *cold* hard concrete
Mothers never knowing how they died because
$1000 vest cams were turned   OFF

Thank You 4 greeting me with a *smile*
HOLA   Salam Alukum   Ciao   Hello

Exclusive Stores   Restricted Drive
excited to shop will we survive
scrutiny lurks beyond each door
side eyed as my feet hit the floor
why this burden   endless barriers
ostracized like diseased carriers

Children should be
Healthy   Happy
secondarily
Wealthy   Wise

White Privilege
    hearing aide dealer   granted **bail**
    <u>decades</u> of health care <u>fraud</u>
    hundreds of victims defrauded
    fraction of *ill* gotten gains recovered
    convicted tax evasion   plea deal
    sentence 10yrs $250 thousand fine

POC   <u>non violent crime</u>   minor drug
    offense   inability to pay bail
    public defenders finagle plea deals
        sentence   15 years to life
    family life ruined   no viable future
    innocent   no restitution
    13th Amendment   *convict leasing*
All About The BEN Ja_**Men**[s]

S
T
O
P

<u>MAN</u>
nip u
lator

MOC
CULL
hunts

a stack of papers
listing 100+
racist synonyms
for Afro Americans
found in a machine
cabinet on the
production floor
of a US government
subsidized facility

<u>**why**</u> do WE LIVE THERE
   wp government <u>**defends**</u>
   real estate <u>covenants</u>
   <u>truth</u> in lending *ABUSES*
   <u>predatory</u> lending *LAWS*
   <u>subjective</u> credit ratings
   <u>undervalued</u> *appraisals*
    Xactly what is it U
    do **NOT** understand

  my spirit guides me toward the divine
  from the shadows to claim what is mine
  on a mission 2 rid the streets of guns
  I am not go n 2 let u just kill my Son[s]

ANOTHER SMOKESCREEN
60,000⁺ liquor serving establishments in America
60,000⁺ pubs in United Kingdom

alcohol abuse only exist in the   ^Ghetto^
is one of the more accepted media smears

Majority of **Alcohol** Suppliers   Distributors
Business Owners   are predominantly white
as in their sister **Drug   Weed**   Empires

Queen Amanirenas legacy   FEMALE   WARRIORS
protectors of the weak
defenders of the Empire

character
is safely embodied
within your Soul
expressed through
a multitude of
deeds   endeavors
passion
cannot be contained

Drugs in the *candy bowl*
alcohol in the china cabinet
existed in small*TOWN* USA
**long before there even
w a s   a ^*Hood*^**

opium   cannabis   alcohol
used by <u>Europeans</u>
for centuries
<u>civilized Victorians</u> used
opium to soothe *their*
agitated **children**

Women of
Student **N**onviolent
Coordinating **C**ommittee

Which...gate
the Plumbers
Gilded Age <u>*gangbangers*</u>
Robber Barons

<u>MINDBLOWING</u>
ignorant   unprovoked
animosity   malice
spewed against
skin pigmentation

white privilege absurdity
2015 white supremacist   m u r d e r e d
   NINE People
   of Color   praying in their church
   police convoy pursue fleeing car across state lines
   5 officers holster weapons   approach suspect
   converse quietly   gentle pat down   handcuff
   retrieve   Glock 41   bevy of ammunition
   silently walk suspect to scout car

2020   3 police officers swarm a single black male
   courier returning to his Amazon Prime truck
   after suburban home delivery   in broad daylight
OFFENSE   parking backwards on the street
   berated   thrown on ground   handcuffed   arrested
   physically dragged face down to a police car
   bewildered irate elderly customer along with
   neighborhood bystanders demand his release
arrested taken to jail   charges dropped   released
<u>courier</u> further HUMILIATED in viral videos

Black white	H		Americans that
immigrant citizen	U		idolize
ME YOU	M		foreign dictators
democrat republican	A		sanction terrorism
HIM *HER*	N		collude to trample

the Constitution
share classified
intel as party favors
mock judicial
proceedings

**WHEN the Narcotics Unit
   Is the Drug Trafficker**

   Who U Gonna Call

will surely   MAGA

sharing physical space
with POC make you
uncomfortable
feel defensive
enlightenment
begins with *self* reflection
embrace inclusion

Slavery to
Superstardom
POC continue
to be traded
as *precious*
commodities

The economic report
from Wall Street
does not reflect the
state of Main Street

needing a credit card
to furnish my home
own a car
feed my family while
fighting for
$15 per hour   a *setup*
for pervasive
Urban poverty

Middle passage
slave trade
12.5 *million* boarded
1.8 *million* died crossing
4 continents colluded
in the African diaspora

WE ARE
NOT IMMIGRANTS

Devil^s Own   showed
their *ugly head*
1500^s 21st century

Divers With a Purpose
Tara Roberts

The BARK
WILDFIRE 1860

21st century MALES living in glass houses……….stones
mandatory 17th to 21st century   dress codes   *the* RAGE
powdered skin   nail polish   gowns   high heels   ruffled shirts
curled white wigs   conveyed wealth   power   upper *crust*

R*III*GHT <u>until it did not</u>   **embrace** THE RAINBOW

religious   political   *icons*   sports heroes
child royalty   entertainment legends
average citizens   little old ladies   A
                                               L
berated   physically attacked   ostracized   E
for simply being born   blessed   X
with tinted skin pigment   melanin   **HALEY**

diversity   reparations 4 self   O
still a threat 2 establishment wealth   O   T
so even 2day must limit full rant   R   S
those n power still control what u *can^t*

corrupt   if a **taser** is a lethal weapon
pharmaceutical   when used by
conglomerates   **Rayshard**
OxyContin Dope Czars   B
$Mil $Bil empires   R
                                         O
Cheaper to pay   O
libel lawsuits   K
                                         S
                               it is a lethal weapon when
                               used by law enforcement
abuse is on the abuser   Crime *asleep* in parking lot
Do Not *rationalize it*   **Shot dead**   NOT tased

living n *the* BIG HOUSE   when the Law is
with a monster   trampling on the wrong
is a life sentence in itself   side of Constitutional
but even *that* **M**other   Rights   remove them
is not going to let them   replace them   change IT
HARM **her SON**

the dance   choose
the most tolerable
politicians   vying for the
most coveted
influential offices
in the land

a Monumental FAIL of late
2016 brought us to
the precipice of a
most destructive fate

IS WHITE A COLOR

if white is so
independently
superior   put it
into a separatist
crayon box

NOW
draw something

when a jaded
inaccurate
reputation
precedes you
targeting
vernacular
hair style
persuasion
garb   jewelry
swagger

B
R
E
E
D
I
N
G

FARMS

children DIE

Puerto Rican[s]
having witnessed
horrific loss of life
devastating
property damage
trudged through
hurricane ravaged
streets seeking
life saving solutions
converged on a
CRISIS aide station
to be further
dehumanized
humiliated
by the *NOTHING
COMING* **antics**
of a *paper towel
throwing* high
level **politician**
enjoying a
Photo Op

BIPOC *true* **patriots**
soldiers   code talkers
RECONnaissance
served as invaluable
military assets **during**
after   slavery

CHOCOLATE American
Champions   Olympians
worshipped inside
the arena of choice

GOLD SILVER BRONZE
US   against   THEM
rising above racism

temporary
inclusion *preferable*
to a collective LOSS

*miles of border walls
stop none of the TONS
of illegal cargo
smuggled through
official crossings*

White House on the Hill
immaculate
Houses of Worship
Fantabulous Stadiums
each a magnificent
architectural wonder

surrounded by
filthy decrepit
homeless camps of
at Risk children women
immigrants veterans
mentally ill indigents
<u>Amenities</u>
sexual exploitation
illegal drugs decadence
immorality solitude
safe from any semblance
of deliverance

Louisiana Code
Noir   1724

<u>Birth of a Nation</u>
DEranged
white
supremacist
playbook of
THIS IS
How^{WE}Do^{it}

S
O
TRUTH
J
O
R
N
E
R

1936 Olympic *18*
JESSE OWENS

#19 LEROY KEMP
1980

what a *hollow feat*
to walk
on the Moon
while hate
<u>consumes</u>
this planet like
a galactic
white *hole*

wp recipe for domination

Native American genocide
enslaved POC
sprinkled with Eugenics

<u>Vasco Nunez de Balboa</u>
witnessed Negroes upon his arrival to the New World   physically fit superior tradesmen intelligent   disciplined modest in demeanor

HAPPINESS IS............

Dear Mama   TUPAC
         A
     B E R N I E   MAC
         V

The
Middle Passage
from Africa
was NOT
CONSENSUAL
nor a LEISURELY
oceanic cruise

Let^S   I^m   H a p P y
Get it ON   H
                A
   G   C B R O W N
   O   K O S I R
  CRAZY   E
You   D E M O L A
Tube   L

national incarceration disparity violates
Article 2   Article 26 of the International Covenant   for Civil   Political Rights

$20,000 to $50,000   spent annually   networking to pay   suppliers   lobbyist   other conspirators to KEEP   ONE (1)   BLACK MAN behind   bars
an aHA moment   yet...

B4 I Die
   Aim high
   Talk it out
   Work it out
   No excuses
   Make or break
   Finish it
   Win
 	
   Excel
   Claim it
   Own it
 	
B the Answer
B Excellent
	Auschwitz summit
	national media coverage
	Human Rights Forums
	   atrocities aftermath
	   survivor testimonials
	   celebrity panels
	   legal recourse options
	
	AA journey to justice
	   ignored historical facts
	   BANNED from standard
	   educational curriculums
	No national media summit
	No discussion of restitution

an idle mind cannot *fend off* the influence of foolishness	**Thurgood Marshall** Expert in *sorting* *through the CRAP* *Jack Smith* **A** *4 effort*

<u>DEFINE</u>
  Black   White
  N word   Caucasian
  Origin date   by whom
 	
start with 18th century
The Ever Changing Lies
	Only POC have
	every aspect of
	their ***BEING***
	reduced to Skin
	pigmentation

they came from all corners of the Earth
to experience the culture of Black Soul
a tribute to Black   Proud   Gifted

Origin of Mankind
Egypt
<u>Mother</u>land

Cats Dogs animals are treated more *humanely* under the LAW **than** POC

Heraean Games *girls*
Buffalo Soldier
   Cathay Williams
Pilot
   Bessie Coleman
The Great Debaters
   Henrietta Wells
6888th CPD Battalion
   all female
Dolly Vardens Team
   all female baseball
Euryleonis
   female charioteer

WILKINS CEMETERY
Dunn North Carolina

Government attempts stymied to desecrate **lost** Souls **resting** place

Tour the nations African American Museums

Henrietta Lacks
<u>*HeLa Cells*</u>
ULTIMATE
<u>**ex**ploitation</u>

Police <u>Serve</u> <u>Protect</u>
Letter of the LAW
Preservation of LIFE
D Elite in the D
Elizabeth Lewis Manor
Michael Crosby

COLOR*ing* sun kissed skin tanning browning
a multi $billion industry why aspire to **BE** <u>that</u>
which the world professes to *detests*

BLACK **IS** BEAUTIFUL

ancient African   skulls were found in California
35 Ton statues with Black features *donning War helmets were* found across   Central
    South America

C
U
L
T
U
R
A
L

SIDNEY
POITIER

Freedmen's Bureau
Authority
Undermined in 1866

MILLIONS in BLACK
wealth <u>*LOST*</u> during
transition to
FREEDOM   *on paper*

A
P
P
R
O
P
R
I
A
T
I
O
N

LINCOLN
H
E
I
G
H
T
S
OHIO

I AM **SOMEBODY**
helping others
    to be **SOMEBODY**
so I can **B ME**

WHO
SAID

<u>*petty crime*</u>
<u>*to Slave*</u>
<u>*of the State*</u>

RISE   UP
against injustice
SYNERGIZE
↑ME↑
↑↑↑ **US** ↑↑↑

FREDERICK DOUGLAS
Douglas Monthly

Brilliant   radical pragmatist
impeccable character

National Museum of African American Music
Heartbeat of All Music   Rhythm of Soul
Virtual Tour   In Person interactive exhibits

Christopher Columbus
confirmed in
his journal   as did
Native Americans
Black skinned
traders with
gold tipped
metal spears
<u>predated</u>
his arrival to
the <u>New World</u>

Oops that was left out
of every history class
I ever attended

the *INVISIBLE*
MASK of bigotry
microaggression

Complacent
Is Complicit
Is Culpable

toe **may** toe
            toe **mah** toe

Shockoe Hill
Richmond VA
22,000 people
30 acres largest
hidden African
burial grounds
in the nation

Egyptians 1st to
domesticate HENS

WE were
IN   Slavery
longer than WE
have been **OUT**

<u>Nuremberg   Law</u>S
Germany

*white privilege
CliffsNotes*

38

Wall Street crime   hedge fund mismanagement
     insider trading   millions stolen   embezzlement
YOUR → pensions   annuities   life savings *GONE*
    <u>GUILTY</u>   white collar con artist **debt** to society
             parole to 5yrs in <u>federal</u> prison
                sentences exonerated   expunged
      white privilege felons   resume previous lives
             new $$million primetime TV contracts
                  house arrest in their mansions
                        tethered to luxury
                                that ought to teach them

   B   S
   E   N a Nutshell   I
   R   1984 | BULLETS
   T   the Coverup   X

     WILLIAMS

         United States Jewish hate crimes up 300%
             Asian   Black   Muslim   hate attacks <u>UP</u>
         what major *race* is conspicuously absent
                   from this list of ***victims***

         Crystal Clear   The HATE mongers *ArrrrrrrrE*

<u>Patent Office</u>   established to strip ownership from
actual INVENTORS   granting **<u>20yr</u>** monopoly rights

     CoreCivic Inc   **CCA**   Corrections Corporation of America
          ALEC   American Legislative Exchange Council
                 mass incarceration <u>overseers</u>

Andrew
Johnson
POTUS
wounds of war

TrumMilosis
inability to
comprehend
FACTS
unable to process
REALITY
aversion to Justice

vaccine   2020
booster   2024

NEW YORK
C   P
E   A
N   R
tral   K
gravesite

A Shepards *OPULENCE*
jet**s**   luxury vacations
estates *$$Mil* facility
Megatron screen
pulpit   football field away
Or
tithes donations that
Match the Mission
community development
quality education
crisis management

TRUE GATEKEEPERS
are humble servants
their Brother[s] Keeper

*A*merican *B*ail
*C*oalition on ALEC
task force

Private Club
members
lobbyist create
controversial
New Bill
legislation
see full list

C
O
L
O
R
I
S
M

Negro   Slaves   1800s
midwife   doctor   mother   father   wet nurse
housekeeper   seamstress   groundskeeper
spiritual advisor   cook   teacher   farmer

NOT inferior   Never inept   NOR lazy

RACIAL DISPARITY
(CA) cultural appropriation

Hoodie 1999	2018 Designer fashion
<u>ghetto wear</u>	award of the year
weave	hair extensions
cornrows	French braid
hot comb press	flat iron straighten
T shirt front tuck	2019 French tuck
<u>thuggish</u>	*designer collection*
bootylicious	bustle butt panties
wig	hairpiece
naturally endowed	implants

imitation is the truest form of flattery
the admittance of racial oppression
where are the accolades for originality
Our Son[s]   were ridiculed   killed
because they were wearing a *Hoodie*

in this moment   my voice is heard   U r 2 R i
ideas expressed beyond the spoken word   f i c
beyond censorship flying high   B the
Day of Reconciliation in My Mind[s] Eye   Best U
seek sanctity of Spirit on road to *Chi*   can B
B4 wealth and impropriety

some do not know Black History   *others* had no
interest beyond what was force fed
settling instead for regurgitated
assumptions   lies   innuendo
as white privilege profiteers beat the drums
to send the collective into FITS of HATE

I CRINGE   MOC are labelled
as architects of all societal ills
that plague the civilized world

YET their creations   contributions
are celebrated in everyday life
SOME heralded as **genius**

POC have always been
the **majority**   If we
were truly vicious
vengeful ***predators***
white power
would NOT   exist

Master manipulator
ordered a **media
blackout** of the
Ukraine invasion
to solicit *Russian*
allegiance
UNTIL
visual confirmation
turned complacency
to revulsion

apparently a
furniture   store
wants ALL
*coke snorting
drunks
poor white trash*
to come on
DowN for **$40**
bargains
African American
history month
Special $1

with implied
white privilege
5 male teens
span the sidewalk
approaching *an*
AA whitehaired
great grandmother

GGMa chose to
stop & lock
the group split
wo further *ado*

*nonsensical
adversity*
STAND STILL
STAY STRONG

white people formed the **1st gangs** in the 1700s
that eventually framed *organized crime*
non white gangs surfaced around the 1950s

a **racist** aversion to contact
with POC *seems to be*
negotiable in their crisis
Front Line Responders
essential workers
emergency response teams
FEMA workers   military

POP	1800ˢ	NOW
White	345t	252M
Black	13M	45M
INA	10M	600t

Pre 1492   100M
1900s INA 792t
SO if America is *not* great
whose responsible

European immigrants
killed 90% of
Indigenous Native
Americans in less than
100 years causing
a climate change

> C R I S I S   that
> **Cooled**   THE GLOBE

cleanup corrupt DOPE
MARKET at the top

NO PRODUCT to
criminalize at the bottom

1850 POC Slaves
were used as
collateral by
settlers for loans
to purchase
materials supplies
equipment
stock   to sustain
white owned
farms *businesses*

Paul Mooney
DL H   Rick Smiley
listen up   straight out
of the Real Deal

Roy Wood Sr
Jon Steward
Stephen Colbert
C J Hunt
RAW Truth

life   liberty
pursuit of happiness
is worth   WHAT

No **O**ne knows
better than the
KIDZS   from
the *Hood*

**Mt Pisgah
African Methodist
Episcopal Church**

New Jersey
1754

WOC
were instrumental
in the successful
engineering of the
1st MOON landing

inroads to increase
POC^S market value
financial strength
are laden with
bastions of prejudice

My father ELIJAH Sansom
Dismissed   BLACK   WHITE
racial classifications
even after witnessing
decades of racial strife
HIS TRUTH
WE are ALL the same
Human Beings

predominantly white
neighbor*HOOD*
confined to the porch
even into my teens
ignorant of far reaching
ramifications of
racial discrimination

then one day   *I had*
TO LEAVE THE PORCH
with a litany of ???
appalled by many *answers*

Eminent Domain   a weapon to usurp power by
subdividing ethnic neighborhoods   business districts
massive expressway excavation projects
disrupt the continuity of thriving communities
SRD   *structural racism   discrimination*

in view of destructive quest for riches   fame
it seems Mother Nature has changed the game
SHE may have concluded with little distinction
it may be time for   Human   EXTINCTION

44

Black Lives Matter   **PEACEFUL** PROTEST against
police brutality   disenfranchisement
National Guard deployed   biased media coverage
under **400** participants   **200** arrested onsite

US Capitol Building   **domestic terrorism**
stopped *certification of national election*
<u>worldwide media coverage</u>   white supremist
chants to lynch **VPOTUS**   other government
officials threatened with death   physical harm
destruction to federal building   property
Capitol Police attacked   beaten   killed
10,000 participants   <u>ONLY **50**</u> *arrested* onsite

leadership   **Bus 2857**   I
quite ironic   NOT moving on bacK   N
that the state   mind   spirit on track   T
of Florida   E
is shaped like   Affirmation   G
A   GUN   of dignity   PURPOSE   R
                                                                      I

Mandatory insurance to offset loss   T
submit a claim or eat the cost   Y
lawsuit a *hot potato* years on end
low profit case   lesser *firm* steps in
litigation meant to make you whole   from African
stalled by *blah blah* until it gets old   Saharan
by the time the case meets the gavel   descent
your financial stability will unravel   *EVERYONE*

SAY IT LOUD   *I AM*   HAPPINESS   IS
THE SOLUTION   CONTAGIOUS

elitist
   out to brunch
incarcerated
   braced for a punch
disenfranchised
   turning to dope
disadvantaged
   searching for HOPE

male arrogance
   typically a detriment
   to Female *independence*

<u>some</u> males provide
Strength Truth Perspective
HEY STEVE

Haters want Black Male
   influencers **removed**
as supportive role models

2024   2024
Do Not get it twisted

elect <u>*humane*</u>
humans

abolish the New 3rd
Reich   INDICT

Georgia Infirmary
Savannah 1832

1911 Maryland
<u>Crownsville Hospital</u>
for the Negro insane

Roland L Freeman
*Times in the Life
Photo Collection*

promoting addictive
behavior for personal gain
makes **YOU** a <u>link</u> *in a
malignant disease strain*

POC street*WEAR*
hailed as uncouth
Ghetto   Until
it became
Urban *Chic*

Challenge the Lies
Confirm the Truths
   back check B4 U hate
fact check B4 U denigrate

Redemption is in order

Natural Selection
renewed all LIFE on EARTH
until the disruptive reign of
Human **WANT**s *egregiously*
exceeded   Human **NEED**

kudos to SB LVII
KNEE **DOWN**
MMIII

Anchor my feet   Lift my Heart   I will Survive
experience the <u>uplifting power surge</u>
soul searching   electrifying   emotional   exuberance
of being touched by Gospel in SONG

retaining the use of 1
cellphone for **1 extra year**
can reduce harmful
emissions = 636^000 *cars*

SB 1070
authority to lock up
IMMIGRANTS
treated like *DUNG*
<u>as was done with</u>
NATIVE
AMERICANS

HARRISON House
LAS VEGAS

STOP AND FRISK
LAW
for LOOKING *LIKE*
an IMMIGRANT
CRI*migration*
System of Abuse

can not go forward
can not go back
dreams postponed
no credit   no loan

YOU have <u>*a power*</u>
that screams   **WE**
<u>Protest</u>
March   Boycott
or Take a Knee

POC   corralled
cattle branded   cut out
SOLD   gagged Truth
Blind Justice

Purge ur Soul
Open ur Mind

experience
the wellness of
spiritual growth
where health
of self **is not**
defined
by gathering
of things

slaves were handpicked
sturdiest of stock
skilled tradesmen
masters of earth science
prior to auction sale

push thru the rhetoric
weather the Storm
POC were *here* **1st**

DWI *dealing with it*
young suburban
POC
racist concerns
safety concerns

HOW
long must
we SUFFER

what is the
PRICE of
FREEDOM

PREJUDICE
complicit wp
police   teachers
administrators
counselors   bosses

No mortgage   No loans
Commune   Unite
with your fellow man
to achieve mental health
physical well being
sustenance from nature

farming manufacturing
service industries
would **collapse** without
a diverse workforce

Brotherhood of Sleeping
Car Porters
Randolph   Union made

120 THINGS you did not know were invented
by black inventors   *mass production is costly*

abuser
pants sag n
bad cop
drug dealer
misogynist
chronic liar
pimp
hypocrite
crook
sadist
deadbeat
parent

**what color
AM I**

EMMETT
M   I
M   L
E   L
T
T I L L

BLM unified
diverse groups
bent on
rooting out
bigotry
<u>in law</u>
<u>enforcement</u>
that may
have <u>never</u>
met <u>otherwise</u>

in stark contrast
Children **O**f **C**olor
must bear witness
to their ancestors
victimization
with **No** apology
No reparations

AGAPE LOVE

<u>Hush Puppy</u>   *origin*
food balls were
dropped along
backwoods
trails to mask
the scent of
escaping slaves

human beings
hunted by
**wild dogs owned
by savages**

global warming
environmental degradation
atmospheric catastrophes
genus eradication

my bad   figment of the
the LEFT[S]   imagination

take the blinders Off
or NO *Pearly* Gates 4 U

Belle Isle   Detroit MI inner city park
2013 $20mil lease to State   new entrance fee
proposal   provide innovative beautification
mecca for family friendly entertainment
projected makeover completion date 2017
<u>island improvements to date</u>
street repair   for annual **auto** racing event

omitted FACTs
Hidden Figures

NEAREST   *Distilleries*
construction empire
real estate moguls
<u>claim your legacy</u>

UNITE against
explicit bias
resurrect
Black Wall Street$

$MONEY$
has <u>eternal life</u>
economic
  security
reinvest in your
  neighborhoods
prosperity
recirculate $$$
in <u>your</u> business
  community

wp diametrically
opposed to an EDUCATED
Black Man

bombarded with
vivid accounts of
  explicit racism
overload   *fatigue*
unable to fathom the
  thought process
behind such inane acts

no accountability
elusive transgressors

READ ON
imagine yourself
  in this endless
    LOOP of fear

Sierra Leone Rising
nonprofit charity

Prisoners
BIPOC labor force

farmed out to
H ypocrites
E xploiting
L egal
L oopholes

white privilege
servitude

Freedmen's Bureau
allocated 850,000 acres
to POC as restitution
for <u>alienation</u>   prior
to emancipation

white bureaucrats
voided the agreement
white people retained
homesteads   even
offered *other stolen*
properties for purchase

envelop a **Childs Mind**   in a nurturing **Cocoon**
encourage *their* passions   a **King**   **Queen** **will** emerge

HOT BOX

T
o
r
t
u
r
e

The ***apparition of Injustice***   named *IT*
IT walks arm in arm with complicit suppression
creating a labyrinth of deterrents for BIPOC
IT will remain a haunting companion
Until EQUALITY Prevails   around the globe

how can a PRISON be an <u>UNSAFE</u> Hell Pit
hazardous to human *health*   *mind*   *body*
<u>**IT HAS**</u> maximum security   24hr armed guards
electronic gates   video surveillance
legal   illegal methods of restraint
restricted space   monitored visitation
Prisoners would be SAFER in the woo*ds*

WHERE IS HARRIET T

The Dark Tower
Leila Walker
Rockland Palace

RUBE FOSTER
The Father of Baseball
B4   **N**ational
League **B**aseball

<u>ecological devastation</u>
drilling   mining
deforestation
industrial fishing

environmental damage
extinction of <u>species</u>
animal   plant   aquatic

YET
media Is laser focused
on civil disturbances by
*non*white men on the
streets of America

at this juncture in time
B   Perplexed

enslavement to
pick millions of
pounds of cotton
every year
harvest tobacco

ROOT of
white power
generational
wealth

*what images
kickstart
your anxiety*

Fill the ***gaps*** in the pages   Book of Black
American History *by whatever means necessary*

BLACK WALL STREET   <u>white mobs **massacred**</u>
Black men   women   children inside of their own
homes   businesses   in unprovoked racial attacks
Black communities were   air bombed   terrorized
burned   over <u>2 day invasion</u>   35 city blocks<u> were</u>
OBLITERATed   ***9000 left homeless***   NO ARREST

Chokehold
Noose without
the <u>knot</u>
more subtle
equally effective

<u>1893 Chicago World^S Fair</u>
civic leaders   promoters
excluded Negro
business owners
from selling their
products
Madame C J Walker

<u>Midway exhibits</u>
<u>exploited BIPOC</u>
featured *stereotypes*
deformed imbeciles
caged savages to
repulse   horrify   incite

RACISM
THE GAME
systemic   structural
institutional   scientific
THE PLAYERS
explicit   implicit   bias
debunk false rhetoric
that fuels the flames

the very thing that *bigots*
have tried to prevent
all these years
<u>Behold</u> a *flower*
of BEAUTY
look around   **racial mix**

POC 3D hair expertise
sculpting   twisting
braiding   designs
 away from scalp
cornrow
 along the scalp
flawless execution of
knot tying   weaving
 artistic   patterns

again
 original   definition
 N word
Circa 1895
 Ignorant   **person**

 Black people are
 only referenced
 in **revised** versions

<u>YOUR TURN</u>   to guess
under **authority** of
 whom   when
 why   where

segregated Black communities
delighted in spiritual harmony
family unity   business success
musical genius   exemplary food
athletic greatness
until
white people craving brown
skin magic wanted   **IN**
POC were *forced* into
Segregation
then *manipulated* into
Integration
to *exploit* their natural gifts

white people
are obviously
terrified of
retaliation
from nefarious
white bigots

far more than
any threat of
**doomsday
retaliation**
from   POC

some   NOAH[S] are a different breed   born to be free
speaking w eloquence to neutralize transgressors
enveloped in HOPE in a not so free country
on a journey of spiritual healing

African American REPARATIONS   in America
that stone is still being thrown down the road

Japanese	false internment
Native American	illegal land seizure
Hawaiian	genocide to overthrow government
	sabotage to gain property rights
US experiments	guinea pigs mentally ill inmates
Tuskegee experiment	medical atrocities against MOC
Rosewood massacre	racist mobs destroyed Black town
Chicago	police brutality against MOC
Africatown	community poison industrial waste

COC *traumatized by*
white privileged teens
bombarded with
soiled diapers
just walking home
from school
SELMA Ala **driveby**ˢ

Pin the TAIL on the
most repulsive
Antisemitic
Misogynistic
Homophobic
Bigots Butt

it takes trusted Villagers to keep us safe
on the ROAD to the PROMISED LAND

sometimes all I can do
while reading this
is place my fingers
across my forehead
rub my temples
with my thumbs

MINDFULNESS *the NORM*
what a world it would be
KORU symbol

Long term VICTIMS
inadvertently take
on the *anti*social
behaviors of
their ABUSERS

A bloody stain on the pavement
Mothers never knowing
how why they died each
$1000 police vest camera
was turned OFF

take your video PLEASE

against the law
stop and frisk choke hold
excessive restraint
your legal rights
never sign anything **demand**
a lawyer then remain silent

Misspeak
unconscious
bias is a
cowards
conscious attack

55

HE SAID *the*
*sexual **assault**
<u>grab</u>* is what **WE** DO
outrage *miniscule*
   define   pervert

yet interracial <u>marriage</u>
causes national outrage
multiracial Child
helter skelter

A **NOOSE** hung openly
signifies a clear
present **Danger**
still suspended past
the 1st sighting
warrants   ire
acceptance by onlookers
as a victimless prank
is a culture
of racial intimidation
with <u>ignorance</u> to thank

IMMIGRANTS
<u>US northern borders</u>
   open channels
   citizenship granted
<u>US southern borders</u>
   families separated
   parents deported
pervasive subhuman
   conditions in
   detention centers

NO rest for the
weary until
unrelenting
racial attacks
are addressed
with more
than WORDS

Release the **BEAST**
of Nevermore

*Domestic   Child
Mental   ABUSE
<u>all</u> open topics
of discussion
Racial Abuse is
still In the CLOSET*

prayers are FREE
yet **priceless**
<u>warrior</u> on the field
still a SON when off
U **all** BREATHed
   <u>Life into Damar</u>

COMPASSION could
have averted the
tragic deaths of a
multitude of other
precious
Daughters   Sons

Infuriating   mind boggling   disturbing
<u>white supremist   spectator sports</u>
human remains   displayed in town squares
bodies dangling from trees   until the bough breaks
bodies gnarled to the bone during slave hunts
racist rants   my school   my bus   my neighborhood
my water fountain   my country   my future

a joke   coming *from* last to the party *immigrants*

If open <u>*wage*</u> discussion
amongst *coworkers*
can get U *pink slipped*
<u>suspect</u> biased pay scale
seek a **UNION** *job*

Melanin   Skin color
complexion shades
not   a SUNTAN

Rampant white
male copulation
with WOC slaves
was the Norm
<u>*never*</u> prosecuted

interracial children
of rape victims
were abused
sold or murdered
by their captors

NO   Empathy
Integrity   Humanity

STUDENT **Survey**
knowledge of BIPOC
history   culture
<u>**BEYOND**</u>
a march   a speech
a street altercation

<u>radical dogma</u>
illiterate   dangerous
lazy impoverished
hideous   no skillsets
short nappy hair
coal black   *subhuman*

www.slavevoyages.org
see database

<u>Hidden Cultural Gems</u>
Robert Brown Elliott
House of Republicans
1871 to 1874

Robert Smalls
freed   republican

Isaiah Montgomery

BILLIONS
  of dollars spent
MILLIONS
  were persecuted
     incarcerated
    lynched
    murdered
<u>all to ensure</u>
interracial children
  would   NEVER
    BE   BORN

COMPROMISE
is a LOSE LOSE

SISTAS *stone cold*   B N *bold*
Leslie Jones   Eartha Kitt   Da Brat
Wanda Sykes   Grace Jones
    Against the odds   Tough
Lena Horne   Ava DuVernay   Robin Roberts
Marian Anderson   Miriam Makeba
    U talkn to me   Get out the way
Fannie B Williams   Anita Hill   Marian
Anderson   Angela Davis   Frances E Harper

Unbridled
Happiness
LMAD   PIR

automatic presumption of guilt
    Awakening 1973

  WHOSE LISTENING   the Ghosts

Civil Service Exams were *previously* proctored in
segregated testing rooms with <u>different</u>
white only test   or   just **pay** to play

to ignore EVIL
is to be an accomplice
to it   **MLK**

We are All
in this Together

1804 Black Codes

1808 Act bans
Slave Importation

1852 Utah Territory
Slave Code

When African Americans can see   feel the greatness of their heritage then they can <u>fill</u> their heart   commit to the legacy entrusted

white supremacy
by <u>hook</u>   <u>crook</u>
1876
stolen election
R Hayes

Rappers are not callous angry Black Men   just dedicated entrepreneurs venting the frustrations experienced by ALL MOC in defiance of angry white privilege discrimination

Our Father who
   Art in Heaven...
if we are ALL
   your children
who Created
   what IS   the
   1 drop rule

*or should I be
   addressing*
<u>THE fallen angel</u>

*B^I^G   ALI   ICE CUBE
ICE T   Belafonte
Snoop Dog   Dock Ellis
Schea CottonS daddy
Lil Richard   Ozzie Davis
Nat Turner   Jim Brown*

AFRICA   **world** reserves
40% gold
33% diamonds

opposition to **CRT** as a standard school curriculum

white America contends **white youth will suffer psychological damage upon** *learning the depths of*
<u>racism   oppression   heinous acts of cruelty</u>
their ancestors engaged in to amass
vast fortunes   social influence   political power
YET
Children Of Color
<u>were not</u> shielded from atrocities   racist *propaganda*
on full display   herald   in Birth of a Nation

Native American children are <u>still denied empathy protection</u> from negative imagery beyond academia
once celebrated Nations rich in culture   tradition
with invaluable contributions stricken from history
INA families exiled to impoverished wastelands

BENJAMIN	*wind*
BANNEKER	*it up*

taking a stance <u>to resist oppression</u>
    Black gloved fist
    peaceful protest
    boycott   march
    take a knee   sit in
perceived as an
overreaction by
  Angry Black People

Read on   Reassess

1 wall torn down across the
    ocean served to divide
only to build others here to
  block inclusion nationwide
Black   Brown seeking to
    LIVE without contention
our Constitutional Laws
        need ***revision***

physical presence *<u>denotes</u>*
your   carbon *FootPrint*
your *Epitaph* will <u>*denote*</u>
your CHARACTER

absentee landlords
  driven by insurance scams
  sabotage inner city
  economic growth
NO plans for
  property rehabilitation
neighborhood reinvestment
  while
white privilege sister
properties thrive in suburbia
  where owners live
  boast pristine facades
  prime amenities   services

BIPOC
exhibit undiagnosed
PTSD symptoms

America is currently
a **hostile** *living*
work environment
detrimental to our
mind health welfare

**Greenwood Ok
massacre
1921**

News Flash of the Day
 WP   OUR MEGA
family farm is at RISK
FIVE generations
of *toil* *sweat* is on
the verge of failing
high operation $$
severe drought

Community response
deepest sympathies
from **BIPOC**
whose lands
property were
confiscated
about **FIVE**
generations ago

Native American Nations
population **100 million**
  rich culture   spiritual
  self sufficient farmers
European Invasion 1700^S
  brought Illness disease
  that annihilated 90% of
  tribal communities
  religious persecution
  to gain land control
POST invasion 1800^S
  INA treated as pariahs
  as their population was
  decimated   reduced to
  300 thousand

NOBODY
knows the TROUBLE.......

what **WEAPON**
can be **forged**
against the confines
of purgatory

YOUR MIND

<u>racist in training</u>
strategies to divide the masses
taught at Jim Crow *KK* Karens place
clandestine groups spewing hate
inherited as an ancestral trait
haunted by closet skeleton reveals
face blackmail or accept the deals
quid pro quo *sucks in* the swine
as radical rank   file fall in line

Crypt of LIES
<u>***LESS***</u> THAN
1 DROP OF
BLACK BLOOD

**NO SUCH
ANIMAL**

Bumpin on Sunset   RESPECT   Little Green Apples
Wade in the Water   Roll n   Lets do the Twist
I will always love U

```
G                    LYNCHED
R          A LIFE GONE    FOREVER
E          WRONG WORD
A              WRONG MOVE
T                  WRONG PLACE
PACIFIC                WRONG COLOR
Garbage    FIND THE EVIL    CONTEST THE EVIL
Patch          CLEANSE THE EVIL
```

JR   H   S
HA   E   L
FR   R   A
WM   O   V
EB   E   E
CF   S   S
SP
BW   O   O
RJ   N   N
FG
      B   R
      A   O
      S   A
      E   D

Dream Fields
Green Book
real deal

FREDERICK DOUGLAS
   characterized white
   privilege as same *snake*
      new *skin*
Andrew Johnson   1865
   Slavery or pardons

Uncle Toms Cabin
Josiah Henson
<u>*unwind*</u> the fake Twist

A child that toils in the fields
   A child of urban renewal
A child of demonic teachings
   A child of spiritual roots
A child in the lap of luxury
   A child in the pit of poverty

each mind
IDENTICAL   *AT BIRTH*
recognizing
LOVE   JOY   HAPPINESS
blessed with the innate ability
to empathize with other
HUMAN BEINGS
Until   they encounter
WHO   WHAT   WHERE

Touch   Agree
U only slow down
when there is no one
to push U forward
I GOT YOU

paranoia of the lawless
ingrained animus by
white privilege toward
an imaginary adversary
of their own making

TEXAS   2022 voting laws
JIM CROW   *add ON*^{s}

THE LITTLE ROCK **9**　　　Ocoee Florida **1**
read history books　　　M　　　　　**9**
by white people IN　　　A　　　　　**2**
school　witnessed　　　S　　　　**O**
the blood sport　　　　S
of racism　　　　　　　A
then garnered the　　　C
strength　courage　　　R
to SUCCEED　　　　　E
in spite of the odds　　 ─────────

research　discussions
will reveal　TRUTH

　　　　　　　　　　qualified immunity
　　　　　　　quicksand of injustice
　　　　　　　　Tyre Nichols killing

I am not going to just let you kill my Son[s]

　　massive ICEBERG SLAMS the Statue of Liberty
　　group <u>out to lunch</u> *exclaim*　***IT is JUST some***
　　　　　harmless frozen water

　　Climate Change devastation　　Narratives
　　　　　　REALITY　ARE OUT OF　S[Y]N[CH]

　　　　<u>REBEL　DEFEND　DISMANTLE</u>
　　　cotton field protest　　　against slavery
　　　　union strike　　against nonliving wages
　　football field protest　　against police brutality
　　　　NAACP protest　　against racial disparity
　　　MARCH AS *1*　　for resolution to restitution

SLAVERY
3/5^s of a person
Compromise
Article 1 – Section 2
invoked by
the *Northern States*

Shhhhhhh
they think we do not
know their children
hear the N word
behind closed doors
on the regular

If I were to tell you
my heart does not hurt
every time I read
what is in this book
If I were to tell you
I am not enraged
by facts in this book
If I were to tell you
this information
does not trigger
depressing thoughts
throughout the day
If I were to tell you
I did not want justice
for every oppressor
and silent observer
I would be a LIAR
      Praying on It

POC denied access to
business opportunities
   government
   corporate   academic
      contracts
business ownership
   sports teams
   casinos   dealerships
   real estate
   construction
   high *end* retail
through institutional
      racism

one race of humans
relegated to
kowtow to another
with less than
stellar character

*can TRUTH be
offensive or just
hard to swallow*

a palette with only **2 COLORS**
limits expression
vision **substance** impact

Freedmen's Bureau managed
100,000⁺ acres of land
allocated by Congress
provided food   housing
medical aid   legal assistance
established schools
for former slaves   poor white
indentured servants

rich land barons   corrupt judges
paid henchmen to use heinous
forms of intimidation to
strip rightful colored owners
of land   possessions   resources

GREG HEAD
Partner in Truth
VENT   Then
proceed to *make*
a CHANGE happen

My head Hurts
DOES YOURS
read on to
understanding

every other product
U See Use Touch
was invented by
or a version of
POC^S ingenuity

sexual assault   *exploitation*
parent   doctor   boss
relative   teacher
coach   trainer
negligent administration

raise the HEDGE
around our children

oppression
discrimination
forced segregation
treated as 2nd class citizen

breeds contempt
breeds contempt
breeds contempt
breeds contempt

protest against injustice is
violence against attacker
standing against racism is

NOT sinister
NOT criminal
NOT bigotry

contemptuous behavior is to challenged

> **HEAR YE   HERE YE**
>
> ***Black Codes***
> Civil Rights act of 1964
> Freedmen's Bureau Bill
> Black Tax
> Jubilee Day
> Jubilee Singers
> Historical Black Colleges
> Redemption Movement
> John Lynch
> Robert Smalls

walk n from the candy store
rid n a 4 wheeler
face down n the street
knee of a killer
can not come out at night
2 enjoy   favorite delight
step n over   dried bloody
remnants of death
on the ground
shackled   mind
hands   bound

*inhumane   ignorant
complicit racism*

human value   character
based on skin
melanin content

a child shall shine a *light*
on *the path*
that will lead us all
to RIGHTEOUSNESS

CIVIL Rights
*the choice
to choose
the choice
of having
A Choice*

Reconstruction 1867
once again   the snake
of white privilege
<u>reared its</u>
<u>poisonous   head</u>

FC 13, 14, 15th
& Civil Right's ?? Act

white **African**
is what race

☐ check *what*

FORT PILLOW MASSACRE
how does the   American military
feel about these brethren
LEFT   BEHIND

Slavery ended   1865
      or so we were told
wp business establishments
Needing bodies   spawned
    mass Incarceration =
labor force *of the forgotten*

       D
   abt it
  DETROIT

B S
L U
O N
O D
D A
Y Y

---

why designate black
when there is no
  definitive
  clarification
  for <u>white</u>

it does not EXIST
bamboozled
AGAIN

Global Warming
the end of the BEGIN
Greenhouse Gases
the beginning of the END
Ozone deterioration
a natural disaster SIN

---

intimate apparel
advertisement
same page
as child sex
trafficking
expos<u>E</u>   <u>help me</u>

1863 FREEDOM DELAYED
JUNE 19, 1865
   JUNETEENTH
2020   *New Deal*
FREEDOMS DENIED

---

peaceful   <u>nonviolent protest</u>
<u>a Freedom march</u>   <u>social Injustice rallies</u>
  containment <u>protocol</u>   *non*white crowd
      route barriers   mounted police
   riot squads geared up   double barricades
        fire hoses   attac**K K**iller **K**anines
another real life fact of biased overkill

The LEGENDS　　　a whirlwind of emotions
Of Soul　　　stirring just beneath the
100 most famous　　skin　jettisons your mind
Black People　　　into a <u>state of calm</u> just b4
　　　　　　　destiny gives you a WIN

jails　　prisons　　detention centers　　halfway houses
majority **non violent**　**low level possession crimes**
　　　inept public defenders　　coercion
　　<u>guarantee profiteers</u>　full prison occupancy
　　　　maximum fines　　sentences
　　　kickbacks to the　quid pro quo　*fold*
　Civil Rights violations　　demoralized　inmates
　　　　　　NO <u>rehabilitation programs</u>
　education　　skillset training　　mental therapy
　　tear Families APART　　due to recidivism

Matthew Henson　　　　THE *IncredibleS*
　　　Vs　　　　　　**t Boss　　B Mackdaddy**
　Robert Peary　　　　smiles when I see you
Who^s on first　　　　*tears when I think*
　　　　　　　　　　　of you being gone
　　　　　　　　　　　　<u>MUCH</u> LOVE

　a Parental Promise
do what you are
　　　　supposed to do　　┌─────────────────┐
then you can do　　　　　│ 55.9 million of │
　　what you wanna do　　│ African descent │
　　　　　　　　　　　　│   **in BRAZIL** │
　　　　　　　　　　　　└─────────────────┘

Safely perched in the Tree of Human *indifference*
high above the fray of discontent
only a side glance at social   environmental struggles
filtered sunshine nourishes   Me   Mine
as we recede into the forest of   not my problem

BLACK POWER
savants of resilence
survival

NO need for *backroom*
racial profiling discussions
because the *front room*
is already On Board
with illegal policies
procedures
policing practices

Henry *Box* Brown
Great Escape

If the Shoe does not fit
DO NOT WEAR IT
we have our video CAMS

Money making Pawns

You are the Greatest
Slave
until THEY SAY
you are NOT

The *devil* walks amongst us
with total command of
True followers souls

I do not hate white people because they are *white*
I detest being entrapped in **the ABUSES**
white people   have the power to HALT

LOVING FAMILY CIRCLE   QUIETS THE NEGATIVE VOICES

> *D* TROIT
> 1837 Conant Gardens
> Shubael Conant
> 1841 New Orleans LA
> Faubourg Trem*E*
> 80% *black* owned
> 1911 Boley OK
> Abigail Barnett
> McCormick

*non*black owned
stores dominate
lucrative chain
stores for
   *Afro*centric
products
<u>proprietors</u> demean
customers
   racial profiling
   aisle stalking
<u>reinvestment</u>
not in Black
communities
<u>*job opportunities*</u>
*t*O*ken at best*
<u>business PROFITS</u>
spent in owners
city of **residence**

Amphetamines
GREENIES dexamyl
outbreak in sports

origin   NOT the
HOOD

ANGELS IN HEAVEN
TM   TR   TN
on my heart

the sanctity of life
spiritual reverence
are core
cultural values
of POC

Brave   Queen   BESSIE C o l e m a n

<u>questionable financial planning for debt reduction</u>
refinance mortgage   *reverse mortgage*
  exorbitant interest rates   equity risk

<u>create</u> a new revenue *stream*   get people hooked on
SOMEthing   **Any**thing
NEW **Law**   legally <u>serve alcohol</u> at *college* venues
another failed experiment in American morality

misrepresented
on world maps
<u>AREA</u> of **AFRICA** =
United States +
China + Europe

30^000 healing
***medicines
discovered* <u>there</u>**
1.3 billion
population

young MOC
standing in front of store
making sports team
fundraiser presentation

*micro aggression
mutterings*
profiled   less than
honorable intentions
just hustlers   dropouts

Be the Answer
PROPS
NOT   ~~ICE~~
STOPS

Heritage   Culture
Tradition   Can Not
be on public exhibit
once a year   MUST
be experienced
celebrated
    passed on
EVERYDAY

just kids loving life
B4 they grow up
to get *Dummed*
D
 O
  W
   N
BY….

products   *UNFIT*
by suburban standards
miraculously
*p*resent on   **URBAN**
store   shelves

an army of **ignorance**
can only be
    defeated by
        persistence
reinforced with
        knowledge
an infusion
        of humanity
flanked by   TRUTH

        I DIGRESS   1841
Extraordinary Popular
Delusions and the
Madness of Crowds
      by Charles MacKay
    crowd psychology
that drives numerous
  National Delusions
    Peculiar Follies
Psychological Delusions

emotional upheaval
    <u>simultaneously</u>
imprinted with <u>ONE</u>
  delusion of HATE

thomas thistlewood
wealthy white slaver
notorious for tortuous
acts of perversion
3852⁺ *rapes*

<u>**HENRY CHOATE**</u>
CORDIE CHEEK
JACKIE ROBINSON
take me out to the...

4giveness
<u>*after*</u>
accountability

Even those living off the GRID
are harassed by opportunistic
        predators

past present   BIGOTS   exploit victimize
    infuse hate   widen the gap of division
   captivate the crowd with racist tales
    disseminate racist propaganda
  gruesome   *postcards* *flyers*   *cartoons*
of grotesque caricatures   *tattered buffoons*

POC are just **reacting** to   THE   S&^? <u>*Show*</u>

No forgiveness *for they know what they do*
I do not want you to feel for BLACKs
I want you to feel BLACK confines
reconcile your role of accountability
with the **Wo**M**an** in the <u>mirror</u>

**CORRETTA SCOTT
KING**

*<u>the Spark</u>
for the ensuing
crusade to End
Civil Rights
Abuses*

Slave quarters
Potato Hole

genocide
Indian Removal Act
1830
   POC holding camps
   <u>boarding schools of
    terror</u>
children   missing
  mass graves
  <u>white adoptive homes</u>
  mandatory Christianity
  void of Indian culture
   tribal traditions
ICWA save the children

it must be LOVE
interracial couples   families
<u>LOVE</u> is a HAPPY place to
reside   in a racist society

sense the calm in
interracial partnerships
diversity *<u>invites</u>*
PEACEFUL   interactions
across the world stage

POC were
B n KILLED
with abandon
Long B 4
B n incensed
about B n
murdered n
Todays
  streets

Black Universe
genealogy

SIDEBAR
   Females   ostracized
  as inept _incapable_
of leadership roles
     construction
     land development
     military
     corporate
grasping technical concepts
     math
     engineering
     aerospace
     science
  woman pigeonholed
disparaged   humiliated
infiltrators of Boy<u>S</u> Club

  Women UNITE
   SYNERGIZE
FIGHT THE GOOD FIGHT

Person of Color **secured**
  handcuffed prone
OOPS SHOTS FIRED
     fatality
<u>forgot I had</u>
   a stun gun
   rubber bullets
   attack dogs
   multiple squad cars
     on scene
   area blockades
   helicopter

    KING
  MANSA MUSA
  Mali EMPIRE

unaccompanied minors
on The HILL Assa9.org
Thumb N Mouthgate

FREEDOMS
  JOURNAL
BLM newspaper

<u>ONE</u> nation
  ~~same race~~
under **God**
  ~~OUR~~ **Father**
  guarantees
Equality for _ALL_
when applicable

there are _MORE_
illegal drugs _alcohol_
  shared **openly**
in white privilege
frat houses than in _**any**_
<u>drug house</u> in the **HOOD**

white privilege   BOLO   be on the lookout
Ivory Towers   ATL   attempt to locate
rest on the   APB   *all* points bulletin
foundation   NHI   no humans
of POC[S] blood   involved 4 POC
sweat tears   POC   *non*violent crime
<u>discretionary policies</u>
NO body cam
stop   search   secure
1642   detain   torture   KILL
Mathias   *theft of* personal property
De Sousa

<u>racially restrictive **covenants**
imbedded in real estate deeds</u>   RODNEY   L
prohibits selling   transferring   KING   I
leasing of property to   Born   T   B
   Negroes   their descendants   Black   R   E
LEGAL WRITS   to   segregate   in   U   R
white neighborhoods   America   T   A
FOREVER   H   T
     I
OUR SONs were   Do not be deterred   O
once *babies*   Good Trouble
the same as   **JOHN LEWIS**   N
any other <u>*baby*</u>

Judge   *ye be judged*
ONE day U might need my **Light**   FROM
to Shine on YOU   SERVITUDE
   to   a   NON
HEALTHCARE WORKERS   LIVING WAGE
OF AMERICA

white privilege
<u>twisted</u> version of
THE   TALK
Birth of a Nation

Sick & Tired
of seeing others
Tired & Sick

Alert Mode
POC approaching
do not engage
clutch your purse
hold your breath
look straight ahead
do not share the sidewalk
look sickened   besmirched
show NO courtesy
even for seniors
store owners maintain
constant surveillance
gun at the ready
<u>micro aggressive   paranoia</u>
why are *they* in here
DO NOT have any money
standing *still* too long
what is in their hands
baggy clothes   stealing

to TRUMP up
supreme being
theories
white privilege
power mongers
colluded to
eradicate traces
of BIPOC
existence
by leaving
gaping holes
in American
history
to rationalize
fake renditions

<u>ANTI   C R T</u>
movement is
rooted in
that conspiracy

| Wat Chu Gon Do |

NONperformance of **parental** obligations
current liability process flawed   deficient
enforce *mandatory*   coParenting
childcare expenses split equally
<u>default</u> penalties   escalate fees   prison
restitution   personal asset forfeiture

77

IF Summer WIND had
bothered to ask his
Pro Bro[s]
watching his back
about racial inequality
disparity   prior to
public ridicule
<u>skepticism</u>
would not abound around
a 24hr AWAKENING
regarding *sanctioned*
police brutality

300 *Black Classical*
18th century
music composers
Joseph Bologne
Chevalier de *St*
Georges
1745 thru 1799
artistic works
**lost   stolen
hidden**

INVICTUS Games
Wounded
Warriors
**Touch   Agree
4 Unity**

reach across
the cavern
of misinformation

begin ANEW
touch
the Rainbow

POC ☑ American
All claims to
Civil   Human
Equal Rights
under the
US Constitution

BIPOC must be relevant
***IF* cultural identifiers
are imitated across
a broad** spectrum
of private   business
entertainment venues

POC do not **yet** *factor* into
Wall Streets <u>bottom line</u>
wolves are busy
devouring more *lucrative*
colorless **prey**

white collar crime

Some of <u>THEM</u> are
incorrigible
savages
anti social
wicked
habitual criminals
deadbeats
mentally ill
murderers

<u>THEM</u>
come in **all** <u>skin</u> colors

*Uptick in
Old Guard
Racist* activity
was the impetus
for *an* **appalled**
army of ***diverse***
empathizers
to organize a
broader resistance
against attacks on
POC   Democracy

HEAR YE   HEAR YE
dreaded <u>food stamps</u>
have morphed
N2   an EBT
middleclass   <u>household</u>
<u>staple</u>   *in suburbia*
now   accepted
<u>everywhere</u>

those   *left behind*
EQUALLY
<u>devastated by</u> ONE
life taken too soon
in an inner city
neighborhood
or
*semi*automatic
mass shooting in
small town USA

Yesteryear
   a nod   a smile   a wave hello acknowledging others
Yesterday
   common courtesy   replaced with distrust animosity
Today
   heads down   eyes diverted   always on guard
     scrutinizing the intentions of even UR own

KIM
could have Ob*tained*
a Law license
by hook or by crook

Character is **Golden**
see Jack Smith **go**

Say their NAMES
Sing their praises

Memorialize all
fallen Race War
heroes martyrs
street soldiers
OF
social Injustice
police brutality
ruthless mobs
R I P   we got this

Love breeds
 acceptance support
hate breeds
 contempt retaliation
evil breeds
 spawns of Satan

U can make
GOOD choices
ONLY if you are not
Blocked from
GOOD choices

AWE inspiring
people march to the
beat of a different
drum   under a
multi colored flag
artistic BEautiFUL
intellGent dapper
charming *humorous*
DElightful generous
flair for originality

ZERO   ROADBLOCKS

deep woods rotgut
bootlegger to
$1million NasCar
Race Driver to
$100million[+] liquor
distillery owner

2nd chances are a *B*
for the **privileged**

the Grand Po Bah[s]
gaggle of
unmasked *ruff necks*
hiding benefactors
will faulter under
the scrutiny of
the coming of
the ....

NBCC
National
    Negro
Business
    League

*Bigotry
sexual perversion
permeates the
social conscious
of our youth
at home
work   play*

*information
accessed
in a trusted
structured
environment
leads to open
exchange
of opinions
concerns*

***do U know
such a place***

POC banned from school
due to hair length
<u>Long dreads</u>
Non conformity to what

<u>IN THEIR WAKE</u>
Unarmed **COC**   *KILLED*

Trayvon Martin   17yr old
attacked heading home
after buying candy shot dead
by neighborhood patroller
CRIED FOR HELP   Momma
DEAD ONSITE

Eric Garner   victimless crime
selling loosies in front of store
PO torture   asphyxiation
DOA

Damon Grimes   15yr old
driving ATV while Black ***DOA***
PO tased   him against protocol
$12mil civil rights settlement
to never AGAIN **feel**
MY Son^s ***HeartBeat***

<u>WE KNOW</u> what
prehistoric animals
looked like   ate

documented lineage
of people beget b4
after Moses

now a **rare** glimpse
N2 African American
historical TRUTH
The Clotilda
HIDDEN 4 centuries

wp *greatest hope* to dismantle
   DEMOCRACY   restore segregation
   best in class *top crab* *cream of crop*

arrogance derailed all campaign promises
   1st term failure   indicted 4x
   sexual abuse fraud *convictions*

   bated breath March To Justice

G
A
R
V
E
Y
I
S
M

exported wp violence from…

| I M M I G R A T I O N Act 1965 | **Children Of Color** **parents killed** **homes razed** **families** **displaced** in 1920 Tulsa race massacre **100 years** later NO wp outrage addresses mental health concerns | save the **white** *Son* *at all cost* SACRIFICE the **interracial** *offspring* *Poop &* *circumFarce* |

Early 1800s   Texas   *cowboy* was a slave name
   reserved for MOC

white males cow herders *cowpuncher* *cowhand*

adventurous black cowboy tales spread thru the *North*
   fame *changed the perspective*

2 MOC contestants
Best Dressed EVER
well mannered
were verbally attacked
disparaged by host
as THUG like
because of braided
ETHNIC HAIR style

white contestant
snidely offered a
Coolio lookalike dig

Viewers lack of outrage
spoke volumes to the
cosigning of racial bias
in American culture

DICK GREGORY
wealth of nature
PanAfricanism

Methadone *man* made
supposed Miracle *drug*
distributed regulated
within government
programs intended to
eradicate opioid addiction

low risk more profitable
than illegal street drugs
know any *short term*
recovered Meth users

Men hanging
in the trees
Sons lying
in the streets
screaming
for HER

What IS in a
MOTHERS TearS

ONLY **1 Race traversed**
the world as a super
predator under the
guise of religion
altruism causing
unprecedented
*interference injustice
irreparable damage*
to **EVERY** other race
culture ecosystem
endless **fact** *links*

Afro *flair* for
fashion dates
back to the
celebratory
pageantry of
18th century
BLACK
Monarchs

Dorie Miller **NAVY CROSS**
nuclear aircraft carrier   CVN 81

Oscar
Micheaux
PTAH
3,000 BC

Nina   Pinta   Santa Maria
mandatory reading
in all public schools

1500^s cargo ships
<u>White lion</u>   <u>Treasurer</u>
<u>transported</u> illegal
government sanctioned
trade   slaves   cocaine
to the New World   *prior*
to the Columbus voyage

I should be Loved
like I Love
as everyone
should be Loved

behold Megan
Mother of
color collage
Now u see Me
Now u see Us

White privilege
Rationale

millions spent on
pretend college
transcripts for
SHOW & Tell

<u>*suggestion*</u>
skip $1,000,000.00
charade
buyout   a business
puppet CEO
child VaCa in Dubai
OH   been there
Done   that

They came 4 the dictators
They came 4 the wicked
They came 4 the extorters
They came 4 the deceivers
They came 4 the egomaniacs

<u>THEN WE WERE **FREE**</u>

WARning
further exposure
to *Truths* may
cause some to
Snap Cringe Puke

wp Headhunters
high school to assimilate
college 2 propagate,
business 2 manipulate,
politics 2 dictate
racism to subjugate
guns to eradicate

judicial appointments
to validate bloodsucking
policies for leeches
thriving in our democracy

Slavery 1863
Emancipation
    Proclamation
Juneteenth
Neo slavery
13th amendment
    to legitimize
new wave
institutional
    enslavement

POTUS   congress members   judicial appointees
    military command   law enforcement agencies
        across the nation have only been
    marginally integrated in the last 2 centuries
white privilege securely entrenched in   segregation
    dominating politics   policing   commercialism
    again   why is skyrocketing CRIME blamed on *POC*

Opioids   imported *across*
    Pacific   Atlantic
wp owned   operated
    port of calls
    shipping vessels
poppy fields n the Hood
are in a picture frame
    yet penal institutions
    are busting at the seams
    with POC charged with
    low level drug offenses
        maximum sentences

white people
DID NOT NEED
A LAW   A LAW
passed for
the RIGHT 2 wear
their natural hair
in any **style**
at *any* **venue**
*with*out fear of
discrimination or
financial loss
            DUHH

$millions$ raised 2 run an election campaign
<u>Redirect</u> *$$$ to* social causes   programs
YOU <u>profess</u> 2 champion   *WIN   WIN*

```
Sacrificing Life   Limb
   for  COUNTRY

     ALI   ALI   ALI

T S     KAEPERNICK   J C
M                    A
I         OP         R
T         of         L
H         HR         O
                     S
BLACK  LIVES MATTER

P NORMAN    VALUES
```

even the ecosystem
has fallen prey to
capitalistic greed
prolonged WARS
natural disasters

where is the funding
*for additional
specialized
supplies   equipment
to fight* massive
FOREST fires

**Is the Truth offensive
or just *hard to digest***

Solidarity
BIPOC **Union
for Dignity Freedom**

<u>STRIKE EMINENT</u>

Holocaust Museum
transcending time space
a **name** card   linked to
a tormented soul
Magdalena Kusserow

L O V E is
the *safety net*
for FREEDOM
spread it

triggers physical pain
mental anguish in its
wake of horrific suffering

average US family
insurmountable bills
inadequate *housing*
transportation
education
medical coverage

<u>deception to</u>
non Americans
on a *grand scale*

Indigenous cultures
survived for centuries
in concert with
NATURE B 4 white
privilege intrusion

1st contact brought
alcohol   sickness
disease   death
to thousands of INA
<u>tribal & cultural</u>
traditions were
systematically
eradicated

Unite under threat of
oppression   inequality
engage *in resistance* when all
roads to Rome are <u>laden</u> with
a *myriad of obstacles* requiring
moral concession to the **T**roll
<u>under the bridge</u>

<u>absolute power</u>
corrupts *even
once*
GOOD people

Emanuel Acho
Racial awareness
videos

LEE KEMP
SCHEA
COTTON
Sports Elite
the pinnacle of
excellence
double edged
SWORD

You Gave It
Your Heart
Then You
Touched
Ours

your Strength
of Character
Wealth
of Knowledge
will inspire
generations
of future
A *list* athletes

Hazel Scott
8yr old prodigy
two pianos
NO deal   <u>Keep it</u>

SCIENCE FACT
melanin   pigmentation
dark skin   degraded
                to light skin
albinism   destroyed
                melanocytes

DRUG O MANIA
begins in white privilege
pipeline snaking thru highways
byways to claim
victims in AA <u>neighborhoods</u>

<u>Passion</u>
a   FEAST for
a IDLE mind
bon a petit

I came as a **baby Angel**   ➤   with everything new   bright
then as a toddler   taught what was wrong   right
N2 childhood   hugs for slips   falls
onward to adolescence   constant flux   many walls
teen dilemmas unforeseen   follow or to lead
young men   women   accept failure or succeed
adults are the caretakers   framing each youth^s plight
elders are beyond concern   of *whether baby Angel*
                is BLACK or WHITE

Loved ones taken from
<u>us</u> by Satan^s disciples

to rest in   **EVER**
<u>lasting</u> Glory   in our
Minds   Hearts

the monolithic tower of
racism must be
dismantled at its core
IDentify   neutralize
 gatekeepers
 promoters
 followers
educate the complacent

Every poem   spoken word
song   hymn   about struggle
written by POC reaffirms
the full spectrum conviction
of   YES   WE   CAN

STRADDLING THE FENCE
can generate
undesirable
consequences
while waiting
to see which way
the WIND BLOWS

POC must contend with
discriminatory
<u>containment</u>   when
viewing MARCHES
political ceremonies
rallies   festive events
<u>restricted access</u>
<u>no personal contact</u>
<u>triple layer barriers</u>

Restore   Native
American Nations
honor   culture
Civil Rights   dignity
Make
America
Moral
Again
Reparations   NOW

A little **6** year old colored Girl
wanted the freedom to choose
to be HER BEST
with unwavering focus   conviction
negotiated a gauntlet of
white women   men
spewing venomous HATE
<u>albeit elbow to elbow</u>
failed to intimidate

GRACED   with a warrior Queens HEART
undaunted   poised <u>within</u> HERSELF
SHE climbed the school steps to
declare   RUBY is in the house

Jan 16 24
Price Is
Right *PIR*
Beautiful
Hearts
Brenda
Wilmer
Made**AGA**

Smoke Screen   sensationalize
drug dealer activity in the *HOOD*   to **redirect**
focus from **nationwide** organized crime
illicit drugs   sex trade   porn   operating from
golf resorts   *luxurious penthouse suites*
derelict warehouses   *back wood retreats*

Run toward your purpose
DO NOT WALK   U might even
have to take the alley

Americas **Iron**
Curtain of **Color**

E
N
O
U
G
H

I want my family to live in a beautiful house
in a neighborhood of my choice
I may build it on an island
it may be located next to you
Simply seeking a **c i v i l** neighbor

Tasers are lightweight   **YELLOW**   unless
BLACK people are your   target   NHI
then you only see   **RED**

Hold Up *incoming*
racist remarks
caught on
hot mic AGAIN

return   Pay homage
to the Motherland
YOUR Brothers Sisters
want to bridge the GAP

Spiritual Hymns sung as warnings   Hush Puppies
Chit*lin* Circuit   Green Book   Underground Railroad

90

Lake St Clair in Michigan during a **Pandemic**
annual white privilege *party*
10,000⁺ boats   100,000⁺ people
anchored near tiny uninhabitable island
law enforcement surveilled from afar
alcohol   drug use   thru day to next morning
OUTCOME
NO charges   NO tickets   NO arrest

POC townhouse complex
complaint of verbal disturbance
2 white officers respond in cruiser
no evidence of *any* conflict upon arrival
families enjoying midday sun on porches   lawn
ORDERED by hold outs from plantation to
get Inside   for the remainder of the day
under threat of EVICTION   *NOOOOOT*

```
I SEE U                  M              FICO reports
CANCER                   Y
High blood         M E D G A R          good luck
 Pressure          V       L              getting
 Diabetes          E       I            inaccuracies
Hidradenitis       R       E              corrected
Suppurativa        S
 Migraine
  Lupus                                    BLIND
Sickle Cell                                  S
                                             I
                   What comes 1st            D
                   chicken    egg            E
                   Corruption Politics       D
    POLL
 gump   trump
```

91

through a child's EYE
a mentor's Hope
an educator's promise

PARCHMENT FARM
State prisons
arrest black males
en masse on
minor offenses
to fulfill Slave
labor contracts
with business
conspirators

| WE STAND AGAINST
| RACISM
| WE MUST SIT DOWN
| TOGETHER
| TO ERADICATE IT

Jamie Pappy
MUDBOUND

New York Central Park
Gravesite desecration
Seneca Village
land confiscated
by <u>eminent domain</u>

Blasian   Black Asian
Colorism   Afro Asian

because we were not
the only people
to endure horrific periods
of history **does not** *lessen*
the devastating impact
s c a r r I n g of
MIND   BODY   SOUL

<u>by invitation only</u>
quid pro quo
opportunities
at the **10th** hole

DO WE LOVE OUR MOM LESS THAN U DO YOURS
DO WE LOVE OUR DAD LESS THAN U DO YOURS
DO WE LOVE OUR CHILDREN LESS THAN U DO YOURS
ARE OUR CHILDREN LESS PRECIOUS THAN YOURS
remove all doubt or you are insane

Sabaneta
Colombia
a **special** little
piece of heaven

Dispel stigmas
false rhetoric
Break down
the barriers

The National Museum
of the American Indian
thanks Frye Museum

B W
 L   H
A   I
C   T
K   E
Quality of Life

Mount a defense against
a life of CIVIL abuses
EMBRACE
    THE TRUTH
    The Village
    The Hedge
    The Elder[s]
MaMa Daddy
Faith   Hope
inject reason N2
    the Process

affirmative action quotas
disguised loopholes to
eliminate the many by
accepting a *token*

potential employees
light skin females
no one darker than a
brown paper bag
lowest paying jobs
rigged testing

GEORGE FLOYD
R humiliated
E shackled
E murdered
N COTTENHAM

Indoctrination
Plantation   Factories
what **man** is my master
to what **man**
am I a slave

<u>Etched in stone</u>
Oldest DNA   melanin
black skin melanin
white lack of melanin
Who beget Whom
hidden archives
dispel fallacies

~~SunBurn~~

How painful is pain
Is it colorblind
How depressing
is depression
Is it colorblind

are u painfully depressed
speak up
Someone Loves You

Pedal BIKE HEAVEN
Ditch harmful
emissions

<u>I SEE YOU</u>   ***will*** open
an inspired dialogue

MENDELS   LAW
LUCY *<u>who</u>*
Dominant   Recessive
GENES

empathy age   nature
racist age   nurture

find clarity in
meditation
b kind b polite
b respectful

prison   homeless
suicide watch   DOA
mental health ward
unmarked grave
DO YOU KNOW
WHERE YOUR CHILD IS

20ft canvas sack strapped like a cocoon on my back
swollen fingers ache as I trudge the cotton bale track
elbows raw   knuckles like popcorn sun burnt brown
bow weevil my only pet turned my frown upside down
endless white mini clouds sit atop a prickly host
face down to the task so the overseer can later boast
a sea of bobbing Black heads breaks the monotony
catching a glimpse of Mamas head rag eased the agony
when the sun comes up there is glimmer   shine
sundown leaves only naked vines   bloody skin behind

Royal Crown of AA Hair
plethora of styles   uses
not just Beautiful
    stored   sustenance
    seeds for planting
    hid alert messages

wp infidelity   OK
sexual abuse   *forgiven*
truth   *hidden*

<u>One</u> Drop Rule   **Exile**

The Sounds of Africa
The drum
Travels with
Kimhass.com

if it is a LIVING Wage
why the abject poverty
food insecurity
<u>insurmountable DEBT</u>
mortgage auto loans
healthcare bills
educational cost
NO accumulated
Wealth
1st of the month
DREAD

Africa by way of Columbia
VP Francia Marquez
Stand Up   **for nobodies**

Negro **1875** Oliver Lewis
won 1st Kentucky Derby
<u>ALL jockeys</u> were <u>Non</u>white **until**
sport became so prestigious
wp banned colored jockeys

JILL SCOTT
Anthem
ON POINT
Lift <u>your</u>
VOICE

A <u>Child</u>s love
natural innocent
belief in visual truths
tolerance inclusion
until poisoned by
FAKE NEWS of
DOGMATISTs

```
J           S
 A  M  E
    LDW
 A        I
B            N
```

Simply ☑ American

Amber Starks aka
Melanie Mvskoke
Black Muscogee
Creek Nation

Genesis **G**eneration
Against **P**rejudice
for meaningful
CHANGE

an inspirational
movement
ushering in Justice
amid intolerance
  a l u t
S to BLM E

only a **tainted soul** would
co<u>sign</u> words actions
of a Signifying Fool
<u>publicly</u> even more
contemptable <u>privately</u>

Deals w the Devil
usually end n trial by FIRE
Ssssssssssssss

DO NOT ENGAGE   *be strong   proud   intelligent*
NO matter the snub   threat   barrier   DO NOT respond
with the same malice as the tormentors *you <u>despise</u>*

Embodiment of Elegance
extraordinary intelligent
resilient   dignified
Do U
RuPaul   Billy Porter
Lil Richard   Elton John
Lil Nas X

U are like no other
U define U
embrace UR uniqueness
NOT *different*
making a difference

<u>a crisis investigator</u>
identifies the
initial catalyst in a
chain of events to
determine liability

WHO rallied the
anti democratic
insurgents
found **guilty** of
*mayhem   murder
property damage*

NOT above the law

THE ORIGINAL<u>s</u>
plantations
reservations
internment camps
concentration camps
<u>THEN CAME</u>
sweat shops   arenas
factories   prisons

**MOST just need a hug
conversation   smile
a moment of your time
<u>hand up</u>** not a *hand out*

specialty Squad needed   worm   maggot
infestation in Cabinets   on Benches   within House walls
eating away at the vestiges of Civil Rights   Freedom

an impoverished Africa
ensures the status quo
of European
*socio*economic
wp hierarchy
around the GLOBE

RESTORing AFRICAS
natural resources to
Indigenous owners
would shift Black Power
into worldwide
economic dominance

current excavation
mineral extraction
methods shackle
land conservation

UNIFY
carry the torch
of camaraderie
beyond the arena
the world is
SLAP HAPPY
when Champions
return *to*
the battle

shows to go ya

W L U A A
O   U
V   B
E   R
         E
         Y

RED SUMMER 1917-1923
AA slaughtered by white
mob intruders   Elaine Ak
E St Louis ILL   Wash DC
Tulsa OK   Rosewood FL

21 other prosperous
BLACK Cities Destroyed

Raw Reveal
Americas TRUE
UNDERBELLY

IDA B WELLS

Pre Trial Reform   Prison Reform   Rehabilitation
competent legal representation   body cams
minimum wage prison jobs   on site advocates
transfer options   *training* soft skills   skilled trades

dismissed SEGregation   to *behold* musical **GREATS**

they came to Paradise Valley   *they* came to Harlem
they came to Bourbon Street   *they* came to Beale Street

<u>Cultural *Conversion*</u>   finger on the button *to*
  *annihilate non*white traditions   religion   heritage
ALL people live for FREEDOM
                                white privilege lives to Rule

---

HEAR YE   HEAR YE
no known historical events justify the
    uncivilized   WAR   mounted against BIPOC
nor has the white race ever claimed the acts of mass
    destruction costing millions of Black lives
was a <u>retaliatory</u> response to Black aggression
PROVING   a white deviant conspiracy exists
   citizens   law enforcement   government officials
       <u>created</u> generations of *discontent*
    having cataclysmic consequences   *to gain*
    wealth   power   *by any means necessary*

---

quiet Restraint
is not working
use Status
Strengths
Blessings <u>REBEL</u>

JIM CROW doctrine derailed
by communities of
EXTRAordinary   *Men Women*
<u>Leaders blazing the trail</u>
activists   scholars   politicians
teachers   religious proponents
giving their lives for CHANGE

inner city Stigmas →	suburban trend Denial
beer & wine store	bar & grill
drug house	RAVE club
dope dealers pimps	cocaine sex traffickers
getting jumped in	fraternity alcohol hazing
layaway	BNPL buy now pay later
numbers	lottery
liquor store	liquor wine emporium
gangbangers	white supremist officials
weed house	cannabis dispensary

placed on a pedestal
ONLY if the purse is lucrative
Brown **B**omber
White House honoree
   TO *social club greeter*

World[s] greatest Enemies
JL + MS
ultimately   BFF[S]

pious civilized *wp*
species cut off
BIPOC scalps toes
genitals heads
held rallies beneath
lynched bodies
reveled in the stench
of burning flesh
hellish screams of
hogtied Negroes
to feign supremacy

M O R E of the ***TA L K***
detained   handcuffed   isolated   in police car
Intimidation   threats to cooperate or risk jail
    sign **release** for police to access phone
         or face immediate reprisal
Due Process   Know Your *Miranda Rights*
        DO NOT SPEAK without lawyer
Not Under Arrest   Refuse Any Deals   *sign* **NOthing**

Zircons are as Shiny as **Blood Diamonds** of Death
bling bling will fade   as did   ONE Billion BUFFALO
SAVE Souls   *sustain*   *renew*   *conserve*

I do not want
an illusion of the
American dream
I want to Prosper
BE happy
I want to be safe
In MY home

Eeny Meeny Miney Mo
Catch a *N...*
original version

313 D4 ME
Kindness   Joy
WE will B free

1953 BAND WAGON MOVIE
SHINE ON YOUR SHOES
Leroy Daniels   tap dancing
genius   *devalued*

cultural statistics
events from
around the world
CAN instantly be
FACT CHECKED

Can You Handle The
TRUTH

BUILD IT BETTER
they will come

<u>every</u> dollar spent
OUTSIDE of your locality
diverts money from
your community
infrastructure
schools   businesses
services

financial reinvestment
attracts new business
sustains economy

manufactured urban **POVERTY**
thru **automated** Discrimination

Negritude movement
1930ˢ

An IDLE MIND is an empty vessel
when *foolishness* gets a foothold
call in reinforcements
MOM   GrandMa

1800s enslavement rape incest

My **father** the plantation owner
My **mother** and *I his* slaves
My father the POTUS
My **mother** and *I his* slaves

Human Property

The life of
Malcolm X

Jean Paul Sartre

Government Decree   New Law *effective immediately*
The Civil Rights of ALL white people
lighter than the sands of Cocoa Beach
are *officially revoked*
all males report to designated prison transports
women   children to internment camp buses
All Owners *of* businesses   financial holdings
real property   inheritance   other ASSETS
physical or implied   ordered to surrender
titles   official documents   to the *onsite*
Police Force of **B**lack **I**ndigenous **P**eople **o**f **C**olor
No exceptions to the rule

DO you recognize *prejudice*   insult to injury
disparity   rage   injustice   grief   anxiety NOW

THE Q   quintessential Masters
of Music composition   Jon Batiste

US 5% of world population   **13th** Amendment
US Black people   **Proclamation**
   25% of world prisoners   **NEITHER**
   1.5 million   **E**mancipated
   22% of *fatal*
      police shootings

     DIVERT   DIVERT   *come one*   *come all*
   To the Greatest Show on Earth   America
   follow the bouncing ball
          magicians   clowns   elephants

A CLOSER LOOK   **Mayhem** at the Globes
   <u>*slap*</u> heard around world   oooh   HE WAS **BLACK**
   <u>*skipping*</u> Super Bowl   ewww   **BLACK** QB[s]
   national gas crisis   yesss   watch those ***pennies***

MEANWHILE   dictators engage in genocide
   murdering **families** in bed   in prayer   on streets
   fentanyl epidemic   national Sodom & Gom......
               let us not forget
   E Pettus Bridge march   US Capitol insurrection
   Death of ROE vs WADE   Right to Right[s] crippled
      runaway Inflation   climate change CRISIS
<u>Pardoned</u>   convicted politicians   friends   *enemies*

     a <u>Black</u> *State of Mind*   is the only acceptable *idiom*

OUR

Natural hair cut off	to humiliate
Whipped raw into submission	to emasculate
Deprived of sustenance	to emaciate
Genitals toes displayed as trophies	to denigrate
Women children raped	to subjugate
Land pillaged	to devastate
Human flesh branded	to relegate
Lynched lamed	to incapacitate
ALL to sustain white privilege	status quo

Edmund Pettus Bridge   line the rails of each walkway with Head Bust   on *plinths*   of all the people that marched across on Bloody Sunday

I am not going to let you <u>forget</u> someone's child

CUT the HEAD Off   the body will wither   die conspiracy to **usurped the authority of MOC**   **plantation owners   job overseers**

now government agencies require the head of households to be cast out for families to qualify for benefits in support programs
alone *Mothers* must *concede to restrictive government oversight that feeds into the cycle of perpetual poverty*   ***at risk*** *children*

Boys not MEN need oversight
both need females as their MORAL COMPASS

Heavenly B L I S S
weekend car convoy of family   friends
headed to the State Park
for   fun   food   companionship

Colored **H**igh **S**chool
1884   Wash DC

The Second Sex
De Beauvoir   1949

| white SKIN entitlement |
| which *sweat glands* |
| ATtributes |
| **make it superior** |

LIFE   AS IN
<u>any</u> Pandemic
UNITE
Erase <u>Racism</u>

IT IS
Okay
to **CRY**

To All of MY SON[s]
character berated when you were created
hidden true story   unwritten glory
enemies targeted you since the cradle
take care minor disputes are not fatal
might be your last   an every day task
in a world where Men of Color come last
I AM SORRY

<u>Household Terms</u>
printed propaganda   they **called** us Sambo   N Word
they **called** us colored   negro   woke up one day as <u>*Black*</u>
printed documents verified African ROOTS
OUR Legacy is spiritual beings   African royalty   American

Mental Health Services Admin
1964 multi million dollar
substance abuse pain
management program
government subsidies
created managed
manufactured & distributed
METHADONE
millions of BIPOC were
supplied with **ADDICTIVE**
recovery medication to
counteract Opioid
NOITCIDDA

LEGALIZED
ALCOHOL GAMBLING WEED
$$BILLION profit margins
Government approved

are POC *just thin skinned*

*try complimenting
an Asian on having a
beautiful YELLOW family*

Betrayed 1988
KKK movie

invisible enemy <u>mine</u>
**would you forgive
their trespasses**

capitalistic
greed an elitist
reversion
to tribalism

Intimidation
TOP *Down*
loyalty
BOTTOM *Up*

<u>**Meat of the Matter**</u>
there is **no** <u>animal</u>
more feared than an
irate wp male on a
vindictive rampage
or more <u>admirable</u>
than a humane one

<u>Gem supplier
disclosure</u>
natural brown
diamonds are
advertised as
amber champagne
to inflate prices in a
market *swayed*
by prejudice

Meditate   Marvel
at the Holiness of the
   sun   sky
   rain   wind
   flora   living seas
   Earth   *feel better*

what HOLOCAST
type atrocities
were committed
to prevent
the **birth** of
mixed race children

| Religious per se |
| is Not *Spiritual* |

alcohol   cigarettes
Drugs to Go
crack meth weed
are all meant
to entrap POC
in a *manageable*
stupor

I guess other
victims are just
collateral damage
Viva la capitalism

ANYONE still need a visual
Slave Gordon
Whipped Peter lashings
Shackles   neck spikes
   full head face helmets
human forehead **branded**
Emmett Till
      funeral photos
Lynchingˢ
   bodies hanging From
      multiple branches
   of a single tree
Dog attacks   human
   bodies ripped apart
      only bloody
      stumps remained
Murder   knee of death
Race to Freedom
   if the other cheek
   must be turned
   let it turn to justice
   for accountability

1 in 20 Black men
over 18 ***in prison***
majority nonviolent
1 in 180 white men

there is a spiritual force
of the righteous
charging through
the gates of Hell
to reclaim   ***lost souls***

the Spoken Word
shadows to light
speak it   receive it
serving with reverence
enlighten someone
with *Beautiful* poetic
healing *Thoughts*
Natasha Sansom

Uganda Mahmood
Mamdani
sites fascist attempts
to divide people utilizing
ingrained prejudice
historical racist
references to demonize
incite violence
to attain wealth

the DISEASE
  racial bias
    tendencies

inoculation
 administered
by Civil Liberties
  Union

A Turbulent Voyage
edited by **Floyd W. Hayes III**
enjoy your introduction to
African American Studies

the *reprieve* from
Open Hunting Season
on POC snaked
its way into *being*
when wp found
free convict labor
to be *less* risky
more lucrative
than feeding   housing
hunting down
field slaves

Blues Players
NEW rhythm strains
soulful *thunder*

Pacification of Aborigines

140yrs of unscrupulous
government plotting
to circumvent
the rights   eradicate
Indigenous People

What are YOU
willing to DO
to STOP the *MADNESS*

<u>South American drugs</u>
are party favors on wp Egyptian marble
ebony wood tables in <u>North America</u>

Stratfor Global Intelligence maps illegal **drug trade**
routes in <u>South America</u>
       who what when where how

YET   in the <u>US</u>   <u>*the largest buyers of cocaine*</u>
traffic routes disappear   NO distributor mapping

National Institute <u>on Drug Abuse</u> concurs
    nationwide supply of illegal drugs DOES NOT
       **flow *FROM*   **the <u>HOOD</u>

Jim CROW is still
   on the wing

> skeet shooters
> *welcome*

DAVID WALKER
abolitionist

AFRICA
Diamond mine owners
1800 to present
Barney Barnato
Cecil Rhodes
De Beers consolidated
British Anglo American
mines operate
24 7 *365*
Black employees earn
25 grand per year
executives   owners
BILLIONAIRES

Task Force Factions
operating
<u>above the law</u>
KKK^*ish*   **S**pecial
***I**nvestigations* **S**ections
STRESS   Scorpion

later dispersed back
N2 the mainstream

SO <u>*The Talk*</u>
safety precautions
still applicable to
divert **a beat down**

judged on the street because I am B*lack*
misconceptions   innuendoes without any fact
my day is spent trying to keep my sanity in tact
no sense of calm   prejudice riding your back

nothing can stop you from your passion and goal
do not take no for an answer from any friend or foe
a new day dawns at every sunrise
take off the blinders and claim your prize
shut out the NOISE and search your soul
mind over matter let your aspirations unfold

K A M A L A   1st
<u>comma^la</u>
HARRIS   49th

Bloodline of
assault weapons
Guns Do Kill
people determine
when   where
law makers
      <u>gun dealers</u>
determine how *many*

browsing through TV
commercials which now
surpass any meaningful
content   finally came
across an actual program

merchandise targeting
is a bigger threat
to youth vulnerabilities
than a Black history class

DO NOT expect a $1000
cellphone gift to make a
child socially conscious
humble   motivated

<u>Black on Black crimes</u>
   sensationalized media blast to maximize shock value
      response based on skin color   <u>*not suspected crime*</u>
<u>white on white   white on Black   crime</u>
      grossly underreported   wp crimes minimized
   perpetrators typically identified ***after*** indictment

```
R   Y                  talk show host intervention
E   O              assess  life choices  mental state
S   U               of a white privilege  middle class
P   R                      drug dealing addict
E   S                  living in suburban splendor
C   E
T   L               friends   associates   complicit
    F                 fiancee  family  clueless
if you will            in disassociated naiveite
   NOT              chime   this never happens here
they will NOT
```

                         WOMEN run
BIPOC HIStory   successful businesses
   stolen   manage dysfunctional
   rewritten   *families with all the*
   rearranged   different personalities
   eradicated   confusion   2nd guessing
hidden   lost   propping up   verbal abuse
                        negotiated deals
√ Afrocentric   balancing acts
   creations   secrets   lies   shame
Jazz   Blues   economic turmoil
Detroit Techno   problem solving
Rock & Roll   shaping of feeble minds
Gospel   Rap   soothing narcissists egos
Symphony   and still achieve
                     constructive solutions

                       POTUS **qualities**

S A M U E L

Coleridge

T A Y L O R   ^tene me et revoca me^
                       Hold me   return me

EARLY ONSET **Rush** to InSaNiTy

buy $1000⁺ tickets to fake event
buy UGLY merchandise to support criminal enterprise
vote for *misbehav^n* political bedfellows
IGNORE   collusion   bribery on the Bench
Fool Me Twice   1 Born Every Minute   1 Flew Over T C..

to those that much is given
if void of character
<u>expect</u> little to <u>nothing</u>

*Mama and Daddy
just made me
THIS way*

WEB D u b o I s   in America POC
are not seen as having legitimate problems
they are viewed as the problem

when *eco*friendly conservation   sustainable choices
are ignored   ozone deterioration   pollution
environmental damage   toxic greenhouse gases
natural disasters   species extinction   *say what*

Job Criteria
<u>attire</u> <u>*ethnicity*</u> <u>*hair style*</u> <u>*gender*</u> <u>*age*</u>
illegal <u>barriers</u> to employment   **on paper**
entrepreneurial opportunities   skilled trades
on the job training   finance paid internships

REPEAL   Archaic Curriculums
REPLACE   *DEAD education Zones*   **Dr**
NEW mandatory classes   3rd to 7th   **Gladys West**
  Finance   STEM   Anatomy   GPS
 The Arts   Robotics   Skilled Trades   Technician
            Columbus has Sailed

  BIPOC and Racism   The EMPEROR
    mental illness   has NO
   combat fatigue   Clothes *or SENSE*
    drug addiction
  depression   migraines   **Believe <u>Your</u> E Y E**
    alcohol abuse
  high blood pressure   Runaway SLAVES
   diabetes   illiteracy   used bulky clothing
   lack of coping skills   to carry *WellCare*
   inferiority complex   products
                                   hair concealed
  <u>staying home</u>   **rice** to eat **seeds** for
     seemed ***safe***   planting crops
       until *Breonna*   at the Roads End

  your *grief* is NOT more debilitating than mine
      <u>Death</u> causes extreme physical
         mental distress in survivors
   has a putrid *Odor*   **BUT**   it *Is*   **colorless**

  National Civil Rights Museum   Memphis Tenn
  Our Father of Peace   MLK   *who Art in Heaven*

NEGRO BUILT

Generational Wealth
wp stole property we owned
making millions off our crops
to buy their family house
that was built on our land
your clothes are our clothes
made from raw materials
grown sewn by our hands
meat   eggs sold at market
were from our animals
repair a tions
can never satisfy
the devil sta tion

pull up by *your* bootstraps
we want the boots you are
stepping *out & up in*
your OLD money funding
elite education has always
been our money because
WE NEVER GOT PAID

Not A ROBOT

PROVE it
Give a smile
Give a hand
Give a
    shoulder
Give a Da*n

Cecile
McLorin
Salvant

STEPHEN SMITH
*Fugitive Slave
Act   1860*

T M Z
*diversity
works*

champion **financial literacy**
share management strategies
digital neo banking investment
never too young

Corona Virus pandemic   spotlight on degree
of explicit bias against disenfranchised POC

Covid 19 relief testing centers   1st set up
in suburbs   instead of hardest hit urban areas

STRAIGHT talk not convoluted prose
REAL pain anguish rising up from my toes
no humor in lives wracked with heartache
opposition silenced in a corrupt systems wake
Oppression
is predicated on maintaining the status quo
by an uncivilized system called Jim Crow
research the facts of POC being victimized
expose crime the government legitimized
with ancestral courage do not compromise
assimilation not an option   GET UP   be recognized

<u>LIFE OF THE PAR*tay*</u>

Bo Jangles
    Whitman Sisters
Jeni LeGon
    Nicholas Brothers
    Nina McKinney

Do not struggle
IN the struggle
Struggle to
END the struggle

minimum wage is a *Bi*product of a *living* wage
which is what % of <u>sleeping</u>   Worry FREE

white indentured servants were high maintenance
they could revolt   seek refuge in other cities
hide easily by blending in with *FREE* white people
hard to identify   costly to track   replace

POC are not in a battle of hate
they are in a **War** of **Survival**
NO field concession   ***level or NOT***

Convicted of Murder
BUT INNOCENT
the Free Innocence Project
discovered
racial profiling
compromised evidence
lack of DNA

multiple alibi^s ignored
sentence   40yrs to Life
Time served: some 20yrs
before charges dismissed

HARLEM
RENNAISANCE
Reaffirmed
Commitment
to Solidarity

G A P Band
original acronym
for *WHAT*

Thriving Business District
reciprocity   respect
honor   family owned
BLACK WALL STREET
demolished

A H O S I
Elite Female
Amazon Soldiers

white privilege
can be <u>bought</u>
then *withdrawn*

so can <u>pretending</u>
<u>to be white</u>

recognize

NIGHTMARE on
PENNSYLVANIA Avenue
Welcome to Our World

<u>*a Black Man did it*</u>
wp rebel rousers *favorite*
callout *to incite the* <u>Reich</u>

WHY are Unions the only organizational structure
able to make demands   be heard by the <u>BigWigs</u>
dictate outcome   *hmm* JOIN
Humane **U**nion for the **P**eople   by the People

116

HIDE & SEEK

Black neighborhood
playgrounds
sparse   inferior
broken   rusty
equipment
you would be
hard pressed to find
age appropriate
multi tier playscapes
sports equipment
with safety
features as in
white privilege
fields of dreams

to evade
competition
is to accept
inferiority

FLINT MI
WATER CRISIS
generational
illness death
100 year
contaminated
dumping site

Drink Up

when the **defense**
is in bed with
the *perSecutor*

watch   your BACK
always have a
PLAN B

riot control officers
in tactical gear
military vehicles
move into target zone
allowed a civilian
white male strapped
with an ***AR 15 semi
automatic rifle***
to split their ranks
to leave the scene
that individual
had just shot 3
2 people ***died***

black man   **unarmed**
shot 60 times
fleeing a traffic
stop rendered
unrecognizable
by family   friends

black child   mentally ill
with knife   shot
multiple times
by *multiple* police
dead on scene

117

Slaughtered
n church
Slaughtered
n school
Slaughtered
n movie theater
Slaughtered
n grocery store
Slaughtered
on the street

YES   GUNS DO
KILL

THE HEDGE
unify to protect the children
   deflect   negative influences
          pain   suffering

THE VILLAGE
sanctuary   build character
instill   hope love courage
teach   truth acceptance
nurture   aspirations passions

MY hand in YOUR hand
is <u>only</u> a *short distance*
from our Hearts

LAWS   in <u>which States</u>
  Stand your ground
  No hate crime
  Open gun carry

Demographic   statistics
   on gun ownership

Ingram X Kendi
black historian
study the **graffiti**
on HIS mind
for further clarity

Indian history   biography
   genealogy   1807
  Zerviah Gould Mitchell
   Ebenezer W Pierce

examined Wampanoag leader
Massasoit
  the lives of his descendants

Sugar
  Chile
      Robinson
ivory keys
  extraordinaire

Discussions around race are so sparse   convoluted
POC must defend their personal space while
countering annoying suppositions

      does brown skin rub off   those your nails
      why are your gums black   play sports be rich
      is that your hair   is that your child
      why are you so articulate   can you tap dance
      how do you comb your hair   may I touch it
      why do you hate the cold   *winter sports*

Every person in your household is different
Every person at your place of worship is different
Every person at any school is different
Every person at your grocery store is different
The difference in POC should not be any more remarkable
Or disconcerting   ON FACE VALUE
then any other Human Being encounter

A	100yrs of forced Silence	T		**Zora Neale**
F	Lost SOULS	O		**Hurston**
R		W		
I	**C L O T I L D A**	N		Barracoon
C				87yrs
A				*Hidden*
	<u>CUDJO Lewis</u>			*Figures*
	the MAN			

    if You Present It Differently
            it will Be received differently

YOU TUBE
Year of the HUG   Best buds   two male toddlers
different races ecstatically running toward each other
Hey friend   I MISSED YOU   buddy hug

TWO <u>Small Girls</u>   black   white   BFF hug
a cherished   makeup extravaganza   playdate
the beacon of innocence
Find Your Light

POC tortured for
trying to <u>escape</u>
<u>shackled to 20lb ball</u>
8 lbs of chains
spiked neck collar
muzzles   toes cut off
forced to walk on a
human treadmill
to break the spirit

THE WHITE HOUSE
is a monumental
tribute to POC^S
ingenious master
tradesmen skills
physical endurance
mental resolve
character under
extreme duress

Tradition of Faith   Tap into a   Mission of SERVICE

Pandemic **S**afety   APB
Beware MOC wearing masks
imminent threat   run
seek safe zone   shoot on site

Or just ANY given Day <u>Alert</u>
eating candy in hoodie
walking on your street
wearing low rider pants
long natural hair
darker skin more dangerous

<u>eliminate</u>
<u>structural racism</u>

support *CO* OPs
entrepreneurs
small businesses
to strengthen
community
economic
infrastructure

Men of Color
3x more likely to be
killed by police
then white males

If u still can not fathom
the Trauma   caused by
brazen acts of
racial violence

submit documentary
videos   to diverse FOCUS
groups **of 60 to 85yr olds**
Nuff said

HEAR YE   HEAR YE
NEW LAWS
<u>Skin Color</u>   not applicable
for college admission
<u>AA natural hairstyles</u>
legally allowed anywhere
*his natural hair was cutoff
at a public competition to
prevent disqualification*
INSULT VIEWED by
MILLIONS
<u>WEED</u> *legalized*
exonerate parties in
captivity under <u>old law</u>

<u>Black BABIES</u>   **used as**
<u>crocodile bait</u> by the
white sTuperior race
authentic
POSTERS available for
your viewing pleasure

White Collar Crimes
minor consequences
*SAME DRUG
possession*
Wp   bag of powder
<u>cocaine</u>   100mg
sentence   slap on wrist

POC   bag of <u>CracK</u>
<u>cocaine</u>   100mg
sentence   15 to LIFE

Abdulrahman Ibrahim
Ibn Sori
slave PRINCE

The 5TH Amendment
Fee Fie Foe Fum
here comes the ***plea***
of a Politi *SHUN*

witnessed   WORLDWIDE
the siege of 10,000
armed   protesting supporters
of *EX POTUS SPIT* on the laws
of the constitution
impugned the authority of
USA GOVERNMENT

The MOB
climbed the walls of the
US Capitol building like roaches
in broad daylight   desecrated
the HALLS that symbolize
Constitutional FREEDOM

Capitol Police   political elite
VPOTUS life   threatened
along with
National Security

shrouded in white privilege
brushed themselves off
crisscrossed the nation
in planes   trains   automobiles
then WENT HOME
masked in everyday anonymity

<u>Less than 60 people
were arrested   on site
Charge ➤ breaking curfew order</u>

unbeknownst   <u>federal</u>
lawbreakers were being tracked
by TRUE PATRIOTS
Defenders of the <u>letter of the LAW
dot dot dot</u>

Convict Leasing
System

Lynch Law

Solitary
confinement
the <u>new</u>
hidden
Whipping Post

Civil Rights
more than
a period
let us ROOT
OUR Legacy in
*Exclamation
Points*

LOVE
of family time
OUR blessing

Africans
in India
S I D D I

white nationalist
pay to play politics

court officials
corporate
executives
media

quid pro quo
cronies
hidden in
plain sight
suits   uniforms
robes   masks

SCAPEGOATS
boy[s] in the hood
dad[s] in the hood
African Americans
villainized

there is <u>murder</u> <u>mayhem</u>
in **USA**   around **the world**
where <u>AA do not</u> even exist

a white LIE   blue LIE
evasive LIE   only recourse
against the wp   B*lack LIE*

AWARDS
OF HONOR

1st responders
TEAM
G O L D
COURAGE
Value of Life

TEACHERS
HEART
OF
GOLD
DEDICATION
Mentors

POLICE for
Justice
BADGE OF
GOLD
SELF SACRIFICE
Peacekeepers

Colored
Hockey
League
CHL

Follow the Money   the Benjamin[s]

<u>Top Dog has the</u> most skeletons
in the BONE YARD

a *maga tude* of contrary things occur in a Den of Thieves
the Top Rogue may be the <u>draw</u>   but not necessarily
the <u>sharpest pencil</u> in the **PAC**

1st installment of <u>reparations</u>
Award POC multimillion dollar government
military   commercial   residential   corporate
procurement contracts
WIN WIN   <u>partial restitution</u>

Living in the shadows of history
peeking from beneath the floorboards of anonymity
shuttered from the halls of privilege
*pre*destined to roam in the bowels of obscurity
think *AGAIN*
UNITE   the prophecy is ***flawed***

1610 recorded an atmospheric drop in CO_2

as a result of Indigenous   <u>depopulation</u>
caused by the   **RAPID**   *European* decimation
of **N**ative **A**merican   *people*
following Columbus arrival in 1492

Married   short black woman   tall white man
Treasuring Life   as it should be in its purest form
*human KIND*ness   *donate to CANCER.org research*

philandereraglephotography.com
captures the *essence* of inspiration

invite to view <u>365 days of Black History</u>
books facts images contributions
influence in the growth of America

Testimonials should stress disengagement
from addictive behaviors so **our** youth
can avoid the trenches of *Long Suffering*
negative karma consumes ALL   BET ON IT

unjustified detainment   rises to level of assault
SELF PRESERVATION <u>triggers fight or flight</u> response

Defending against oppression
is not an act of aggression   or criminal

Cultural Heritage   *indigenous people as well*
as Black slaves from Africa
produced <u>Medicines</u> from <u>natural herbal sources</u>

ONE cure stopped the spread of SMALLPOX
In the New World

<u>N</u>
<u>E</u>   SLAVERY
<u>O</u>

Will Pickett created
<u>*steer*</u> <u>wrestling</u>
using his TEETH

Mahatma Gandhi   Martin Luther King Jr
Nelson Mandela

Malcolm X fmr Malcolm Little
Cassius Clay fmr Muhammad Ali

Frontline Warriors *then now*
Desmond Tutu   14th Dalai Lama
John Lewis
ALL BROUGHT US CLOSER
to *this* New Day of HOPE

<u>resilience integrity fortitude courage</u>
pass the baton of business savvy to others
seeking a firm foothold on the slippery
slopes to financial security

mentorship   helps to narrow objectives
prevent redundancy in strategic planning

W
I
H E   RO
L
L OV E
4
EVER

Georgia Infirmary
1832

SOCIAL CHANGE <u>Can Not</u>   happen
unless status quo is ***DISRUPTed***

OR   The Speech   1715
by Willie Lynch   *Will Prevail*

CDSV   Capitalist Death Squad Vultures
circled the day after the **Maui** calamity amid
Monumental Human Suffering   Despair
to steal heritage   family properties for ***pennies***

UNFANTHOMABLE gall
    freefall into the abyss of tone death GREED

<u>Brain Food</u>
Toni Morrison
   James Baldwin
ObamaS

Non fiction genres
cultural   history
poetry   politics
social issues
lessons learned

let me get this
straight it is OK to
exploit *MY* MoMs
affliction *in a
cowardly blindsided
personal attack*
to entertain millions
*under the
guise of a JoKe*

ego   or   envy

**BENEFITS *of living*
<u>OFF</u>   *the* GRID**

Penal Labor
UNICOR

indecision teeters on the edge of
shoulda   woulda   coulda
a passion ignored   a dream deferred

Do Not be deterred express your opinions
pursue your passions display your gifts
behold GREATNESS

POTUS *of old*   G   Benjamin
215lbs   R   SINGLETON
     O   Kansas
D *SEAN* REED   U   EXOdusters
Gun   P

think

National Memorial for Peace and Justice
800 lives hanging by a thread
sheer terror driven by the presumption of guilt
<u>*why* go see it</u>   because it is as **shockingly
unbelievable** as the Grand Canyon **end to end**

a Woman's instinct to protect the innocent
specifically the overall health   welfare of children
is even <u>*more*</u> inherent
than a man's drive for power   sex

sacrificial lamb   WHEN tested

<u>*what*</u> is   JAY Z   ***B*** slapped   The Academy
Sexier   in defense of his beloved
<u>*when*</u>   Wife's <u>Genius</u>   <u>NO Ban imposed</u>
it comes   LOVE over Rudeness
in   The Queen Rocks
BLACK   *The King*   Chivalry Rules

everyone pushed the envelope
>   things got out of hand
nature is on the war*path*
>   when you stress the land
every man woman child
>   has the option not to defile
but we looked the other way
>   chose not to reconcile
it was given to us on the 3rd day
magnificence N2 landfills   now we must pay
we still have options if we commit
>   stop the desecration 4 everyone^s benefit
reconsider moving forward
>   4 only personal gain
if a child can NOT go outside 2 play
>   how will we explain
we must protect this sacred place
Mother Earth provides 4 the human race
the damage is at a critical stage
>   almost to a point of no return
reverse the current trend
>   make it your #1 concern
or continue the carnage   live forever in fear
as field foul water life rapidly disappear

African slave metallurgist in Jamaica invented
wrought iron   high tensile steel   <u>Henry Cort</u>
<u>Europeans</u>   kidnapped inventors   stole technology

Apartheid *in the land of the free* is beyond understanding

>   now even <u>you</u> know enough
> to do *something* **positive to dismantle it**

top 10% **Bull** market on **Wall Street** while 42 million
people received meager unemployment benefits
prices skyrocket retail sales *all* time Low
oil supply reduced to a negative margin
personal income savings obliterated
much like the homes in Midland MI ***flood***

stock manipulation of money market transfers
benefit <u>white privilege</u> *elite* Capitalism hawking 5.0

DRED SCOTT	Mass Media coverage focused on saving pennies at the gas pump **1** of many diversions to deflect from BILLIONS scammed from overpriced
US citizen *OR NOT*	transportation household goods baby formula medical services housing *high tech* products
FREDERICK DOUGLAS	Ergo subjugation breeds despair and desperate acts

name 13 Black millionaires billionaires	1881 E E WARD
name 13 US President^S US Justice^S that were <u>**slave owners**</u>	Moving Storage

SO THREATENED white power created walls clubs
networks glass ceilings social media platforms
to defuse female intervention in a Man^S world
but it is ***nothing*** *not anything* wi.........
<u>women drive the train ***even*** from the caboose</u>

Nelson M A N D E L A
a *BODY*
was imprisoned
NOT a **MIND**

Humanitarian Crisis^
exist in America TOO
Fly <u>your</u> Flag
Upside down

RACISM

D C G
R H A
I   I   M
N L B
K D L
I   R   I
N E N
K N G
G ∞
 S E X

KIDS are
surrounded

AWAKENING

    E   I
 H Hoodwinked   N
T   Compromised   G
     Bamboozled
     Blind Sided
Looped Out of your Birthrights
into *programmed* bondage
RESEARCH DISCOVER REBOOT

Mental Health professional
onsite for <u>Mental Health Crisis^</u>

> share community issues   resolve concerns
> through internal discussions
>
> <u>disregard</u> sparse   invalid information
> *force fed* from a white privilege perspective
> those **controlling** the narrative   remain *suspect*
> in the factual nature of the message

      micro aggression to physical abuse
              racially inflicted PTSD
  paralyzes   motivation
  inhibits   critical thinking
  triggers   anxiety fight or flight
  shadow boxing   faceless bigotry

  Slave Mentality **begins**   **ends with**
  the power afforded *the oppressor*

      STORER College   HARLEM
    National Association
     Of Colored Women   *H* *G*
                                      e   l
    Niagara Movement   l   o
                                      l   b
                                      f   e
                                      i   t
                                     g   r
  Mass graves   hidden burial grounds   h   o
  <u>**beneath**</u>   t   t
     mounds of overgrown weeds   e   t
     statutes of racist   r   e
     architectural wonders   *s* *rs*
  are SANCTIFIED grounds *nonetheless*

  DEMAND historical site recognition
       timelines to facilitate an
       official ancestral registry

EMINENT DOMAIN
Tennessee   2023   a newly built white owned
business complex wanted to have direct access
to the main highway
without compensation a center parcel of a
Black **F**armers land was confiscated   excavated
paved to allow for a new straight road

another wp conspiracy
chokehold on AA generational wealth

LOW RIDERS   cultural engineering marvels
artistic prowess in *self* expression

CHICAGO CALUMET heritage area
OPENLANDS projects   people   places   events
<u>*Physical   AA heritage Water Trails*</u>
   Battle of Palmita Ranch
   New Jersey Black Heritage Trail
   Chicago South Ton Farm
   Marina for black residents
   Beaubien Woods to Robbins Village
   Nora Neale Hurston Dust Track
   Fort Pierce FL trail
<u>*Virtual African American historic trails*</u>
   African American trail project
   Dorchester N burial grounds Malcolm X
   Ella little Collins house   Roxbury Boston
   California AA freedom trail
   Emancipation National Historic trail

BLACK MADONNA

MOTHER to **every** child
from the big house to the White House
nurture   preach
at every twist   turn   we must teach
through the streets as in the fields
lead danger from innocents like Emmett Till
protect the black male child adopted or conceived
lest the 100 year master plan will leave us bereaved
our empathy is inherent   curse or gift
power   pride have set men adrift
females instinctively protect all life
*non*violence can end dissension   strife
not a conductor of confusion blame or hate
just persistent on the path that shapes your fate
Inclusion   I am you   you are me by design
embrace the true essence of *Human* KIND

Mothers enveloped in Love   Faith   Inclusion
that No foe to Democracy can penetrate
No tyrant can regulate
No military might can separate
No law can eradicate

WE ARE UNITED

I am not going to just let you kill my Son[S]

EPILOGUE

Black and Indigenous People of Color Decree for Justice:

A subversive amoral consciousness prevails within the white race. The institution of racial discrimination, its founders and complicit followers are herein charged with <u>defrauding</u> the public by establishing an elitist society that undermines the set of beliefs of a formerly egalitarian 1600s society.

The anti-Black segments of society colluded with landowners, slave traders, government and law enforcement to deprive, displace, dispossess, and enslave Black & Indigenous People of Color (BIPOC). False narratives were used to create a cult following to advance the theory of a multi-race society consisting of superior beings and sub*human* species, while knowing the claims to be erroneous.

White privilege engaged in
- obstruction of justice: impede, injure, threaten, and oppress persons in their free exercise and enjoyment under the 14th amendment, Civil/Human Rights Laws and Laws of Nature.
- Violating POC's constitutional rights and denying equal opportunity for centuries, even after the 1863 Emancipation Proclamation.
- A divisive conspiracy that evolved into a national, racially motivated crusade responsible for the demise of millions.
- Recruiting an anti black federation to commit acts of fraud, deceit, and persecution of non-white races.
- Subverting democracy to stay in power through sadistic and seditious acts against humankind.

Thereby, all guilty perpetrators are liable and subject to prosecution for these alleged crimes. Heinous subversive acts include, but are not limited to:

Involuntary transport of human beings	Bondage
Creating caste system	Apartheid
Jim Crow laws	Black codes
False imprisonment	Mass incarceration
Vagrancy laws	Separate but Unequal Laws
Racial covenants	Redlining Blacklisting
Color Quotas	Manufactured poverty

In the court of opinion condemning apartheid and other copious crimes against Civil & Human Rights, white privilege has been found guilty. Penalties and conditions for the purpose of making victims whole will include:

1. <u>Restitution</u> to be determined by a tribunal. Past transgressions cannot be forgiven simply because they have been ignored. Healing is in the acknowledgement of the act and sincerity to repent.
2. <u>Reparations,</u> shall begin with a smile and symbolic shaking of hands with every Person of Color & Indigenous Native American during an initial meeting.
3. A written public apology to victims and their heirs for acts of racial discrimination outlined above.

Charges not addressed, in writing, within 30 days will be construed as an admission of guilt, to be used as evidence in future liability claims.

About the Author

My name is
Lorna D Whitfield
"Cookie" (Sansom)

Great Great Grandmother ∞
Servant   Author   Poet

1ˢᵗ Female African American
Journeyman Electrician
at
Detroit Newspapers Agency   IBEW
Steward Local #58

Los Angeles Times   IBEW

General Dynamics Tank Plant   UAW

Peerless Gear and Machine   UAW

1ˢᵗ Female African American
Apprentice Electrician
General Motors Corporation
Hydramatic Transmission Div   UAW

Other Literary Works

COLOR ME BLACK

https://thetravelerweekly.com/2020/07/16/color-me-black

Made in the USA
Middletown, DE
07 February 2025